THE JANES

B.M. Hardin

ISBN-13: 978-1545386965
ISBN-10: 154538696X

This book is a work of fiction. Any similarities of people, places, instances, and locals, are coincidental and solely a work of the authors imagination.

Dedication & Thank You's

I truly thank the Man above for my gift and for the opportunity to live in my purpose and the courage to chase after my dreams.

I thank my readers for following my work and allowing me to entertain them time and time again. I appreciate their continuous support and their interaction with me daily in my book club: "It's A Book Thing"

I appreciate you ladies more than you know!

This book is dedicated to all of my readers, family and friends, that continuously listen to my book ideas and share their opinions, good or bad. I am who I am, because of ALL OF YOU! THANK YOU!

The Janes

CHAPTER ONE

"Someone is following me."

"What?"

"I know it sounds strange, but for the last few days…it's just this feeling," I said to my husband, glancing behind me again, just before I entered the coffee shop.

"What are you talking about Jane? Who would be following you?"

"I don't know. No one I suppose. Maybe I'm just on edge from the burglaries that's been happening near our condos lately."

"Yeah. Maybe. Well, if you get some down time today, maybe you should look at a few listings."

"I'll try. The sooner we find a house, the better."

"Right. Because then…it's baby-making time," Brice cheered.

"Humph, just plain ole' nasty," I giggled.

"Can we do something nasty later?"

"Sure. First, I'm going to take off all of my clothes, slowly. You're going to ask to touch me, but I'm going to make you wait. Then, ohhh, then I'm going to walk into the bathroom, sit on the toilet…and then I'll call you when it's time to wipe my ass. Oh, yeah baby, nice and nasty," I snickered.

"Damn. You sure know how to soften up a hard dick," Brice grunted.

"Thanks for the compliment, baby," I laughed at him, as I approached the counter.

"Anyway, I'll call you once I make it to the office. I love you. Bye," I said, smiled at the cashier and placed my order to go.

"Excuse me. It wasn't my intention to eavesdrop, but I overheard you say that you were looking for a house. If you want, I can give you my realtor's card. She's really good," the lady behind me said, pulled out her wallet and handed me a card.

"Thank you."

"No problem. I'm sure that she will be able to find you something," she assured me, as I got my coffee and she stepped up in line. I tucked the card into my purse and headed out of the door in a rush.

I checked my surroundings, just to see if I saw anything out of the *norm*.

"Jane, no one is following you. Get yourself together," I scolded myself aloud for being paranoid. In a rush to beat the morning traffic, I hopped into my car and pulled off, but not before I noticed the lady who handed me the card coming out of the coffee shop…without a coffee, or anything else for that matter.

Hmm…I guess she changed her mind.

~***~

We turned down a street called S.J. Lane.

I squealed once we stopped in front of a big white and yellow house with the cutest little porch swing.

Big, green, oak trees swayed gracefully all around us and it seemed as if the sun was shining just a little bit brighter on the house that we were there to see.

"I love it already," I whispered to myself.

Studying the other houses on the street, I noticed that all of them looked the same. Every single house was the same color, same build, same curb appeal and even the same exact flowers---including the one that we were there to see. I wasn't a fan of blending in, but luckily, giving things a little bit of "flavor" was my specialty.

The realtor waved and headed in our direction.

"Hi Guys! We've been talking for weeks, but it's nothing like putting faces with names---or should I say faces with voices? Anyway, you must be Brice. And you my dear, must be Jane," she said and extended a hand.

"Actually, it's Mary Jane, but I go by Jane, for short," I said to her. The grin on her face disappeared, for only a second, but she quickly recovered it.

"Right. Of course, you do. Shall we?"

My husband grabbed my hand, and she led the way.

For the next thirty minutes, or so, we toured every inch of the house and I imagined what it would feel like to live there for the next thirty years or so. And though this was the very first house that we were seeing, in person, in my opinion, it was perfect.

"This house is breathtaking! Not to mention that it's in one of the best neighborhoods in this city. And the people around here are so nice and friendly. You'll love it here. I'm sure of it! So, let's hear your thoughts. What do you think?"

Brice grinned at me and I nodded my head.

This was it. This was the house that I was supposed to raise my family in and grow old and grey with the man of my dreams.

Brice and I have only been married for a little over a year ago, but we'd been together forever. We were high school sweethearts. And from high school, we went to the same college, graduated and then we went straight to work. But finally, we tied the knot and now we were ready for the next chapter and though usually we took our time about making decisions, this house, and the timing, just felt right. Besides, it was a must that we get out of our condo since it had been broken into only days before.

I smiled at the children's toys all over a few of the freshly mowed lawns. I inhaled the fresh scent of flowers and I could smell the water from the pools.

Yes. This was the house, this was the neighborhood, that I'd been looking for.

I squeezed Brice's hand and he opened his mouth.

"We'll take it."

The realtor shrieked and as we walked to our car, she chatted about the paperwork and the process.

I glanced at the house next door. The curtain moved as the figure stepped back from the window. I watched the window, waiting for someone to reappear, but they never did. But as we drove away, I couldn't stop smiling. I had a gut feeling that from that day forward, things for us, would never be the same. And to date, I was proud to say that my gut had never steered me wrong.

At least not yet.

~***~

"I think we should give this bad boy one last hoo-rah before we go," Brice said tapping on the island in the center of the condo's kitchen.

Finally, it was moving day! We'd found the perfect house over two months ago, but as of last week, it was officially ours and I was happier than ever!

Brice kissed my cheek as I shook my head.

"Oh no, Brice, no we don't have time for that. The movers will be here in any minute, and I still need to finish up a few things," I giggled.

"All I need is five minutes; three, if you participate," Brice grinned slyly and with one quick motion, he picked me up and I locked my feet around his waist.

"No one is as sweet," he kissed me. "No one is as sexy," he kissed me again. "No one is more beautiful," Brice grinned as I beamed at him. "No one is more right for me, than you. I love you," he whispered.

"You better," was all I could say before he devoured my lips. And before we knew it, five minutes had turned into more like forty-five and we found ourselves scurrying to pull ourselves together as the movers banged on the front door.

Once Brice and the other men got busy loading the cars and truck, I headed to look over my plans.

I was an interior designer. I owned my own company, which was in the process of something like a merger. About a year ago, I'd reconnected with my good friend and college roommate, Charity, who was also a successful interior designer. Once we were back in touch, we started to work on a few projects together and over time, we discovered that we made one hell of a team.

So, we decided to partner up.

And since her space was bigger, I was moving to her location, which was conveniently located in the same city as our new house.

We were moving from Raleigh, North Carolina to a very small city called Smithfield. And let me tell you, it was a big difference from what we were used to.

It was what we called *country*---and I'm talking about well water drinking, biscuits and molasses eating, barefoot walking, houses miles apart living…country!

Luckily, the realtor was familiar with the area and per my request, she found a few available listings, in the few flourishing, and updated communities of the small town. And our house just happened to be in one of them.

Charity lived in the town of Cary. She refused to live in Smithfield, even though her business was there. She'd simply said that the location space was cheaper and that she was always needed in a town that was so dated. I was just thankful that we'd found a house so close to my job; though Brice hadn't been so lucky.

Matching my artistic side, Brice was a well-known graphic designer and though his business was going to remain in the Raleigh-Durham area, he'd said that he didn't mind driving forty-five minutes to an hour to work every day.

"Ready?" Brice finally said about an hour later.

I followed Brice to the front door. I looked behind me one last time. "Ready."

And after an hour trip, turned into more like two, due to traffic, finally, we arrived at our new home.

"Aww, look, someone left us something," I squealed. There was a big basket, full of goodies and balloons sitting on the first step of the front porch. Brice got out of his car and immediately started to unload.

It was a beautiful Saturday and as I made my way to the trunk of the car, my heart fluttered at the sound of children's laughter. I looked around. I could hear them. But I couldn't see them; which surprised me being that it was now the beginning of summer. But the streets were surprisingly empty. Still, the sounds of their giggles warmed my heart.

I watched Brice reach for another box and finally, I reached for my first one. Our wedding picture was on the top of it and I traced the outline of Brice's face with my finger. At that very moment, I felt nothing but gratitude.

I was happy. I was content.

I smiled, grabbed the box and turned around.

"Ahh!"

I dropped the box and clutched my chest.

It was a woman. Latino maybe. Dark hair and dark eyes, just standing there, right behind me.

She didn't say anything or react to my fright. She just stood there and smiled.

Where in the hell did she come from?

We just looked at each other for a while. Finally, she spoke. "Here you go," she said, reaching me the fruit basket that she was holding in her left hand.

"Thank you," I managed to say and I took the basket from her.

Without saying anything else, she knelt to the ground to gather the broken glass from the picture frame that had fallen off the top of the box.

"Oh no, I can get that," I said sitting the basket in the trunk of the car and then squatting down beside her to help.

She didn't say anything to my comment. Instead, she started to hum as she picked up the glass in a hurry.

"You look happy on this picture," she commented, stopping for only a second to observe our wedding photo.

"I was. And happy is an understatement. I was ecstatic! My wedding day was the best day of my life. It was the day that I married my best friend," I beamed.

"Your husband is your best friend?" She asked almost in disbelief.

I looked down at the huge wedding ring on her finger. "Yes. Isn't yours?"

She made a funny face and then she laughed. "Not even close. But I'll buy you a new picture frame."

"No need. I have plenty of them as wedding gifts that we haven't used yet." She nodded at my reply.

"Well, allow me to introduce myself. I'm Jane," she flashed her beautiful white smile, as she stood up.

"Really? I'm Jane too. How cool is that?" I said to her. I guess I could've included Mary, but I preferred to be called just Jane anyway.

Once I was on my feet, she reached out her hand for me to shake it.

"Oh, you have a piece of glass stuck in your finger," I pointed out. She looked at her hand surprised.

"Hmm…I didn't even feel that," she shrugged, but she never bothered to remove the glass. Instead, she eyed the blood that was starting to drip, hungrily. As though she wanted to lick it or something, but thought that it would be rude. When she noticed that I was watching her, she grinned and then she spoke, fast, as though she was suddenly in a hurry. "Well, nice to meet you Jane. I hope you enjoy the basket. I should get home, and take care of this," she wiggled her finger and then she turned her back to me.

I watched her walk away. And what a funny walk it was! Both of her arms were straight down, by her side, as she somewhat walked and skipped, at the same time; from left to right. It was one strange ass walk and weird as hell to watch. I caught myself leaning my head to the side as I watched her. I waited to see which house she went into. She lived about three houses down, on the other side of the street. I was surprised that I hadn't seen or heard her coming in my direction.

"Uh oh, you have got to be the clumsiest person that I know," Brice joked.

"Shut up, and pick up the box."

I showed him the gift basket.

"This came from one of our neighbors. And guess what, her name is Jane, too," I said following behind Brice towards the house.

"Really? That's funny because the basket that was on the front porch, with the balloons, also said that it was from "Jane"," he said as though he was amazed.

Hmm… I've never known Jane to be such a popular name.

~***~

"Busy day?"

"Yes. Charity should be here shortly to help me get started on a few things."

"Okay. Make it look nice for big *daddy*. I love you," Brice chuckled and kissed my forehead.

"You better. Have a good day at work," I shouted behind him as the front door closed.

I walked around the living room, imagining how it was going to look once everything was finished and in place. My creative and artistic juices were flowing and my thoughts were of colors and patterns until the sound of the doorbell stole my attention.

I headed towards the front door.

"He must've forgotten something," I mumbled but as I opened the door, to my surprise, it wasn't Brice at all.

"Hello."

"Hi," I greeted the group of ladies that were standing on the porch in dresses and smiles. One of them was holding a pie that immediately made my mouth start to water.

"This little baby is for you. It was made with fresh picked cherries and a whole lot of love. We just wanted to come by and welcome you to the neighborhood," the blonde lady in the middle said as she reached me the pie.

I stared at them. It was strange how much they all sort of matched; same dresses, same hairstyles, same funny looking grins.

"Thank you for the pie. It smells so good."

"You're welcome. All settled in?"

"Oh, no. We have a long way to go. I'm just about to get started with decorating the living room."

"Oh. I know this really good decorator…"

"Oh no. I'm doing it myself, with a friend. It's kind of my thing. I'm an interior designer," I beamed proudly at them but for a second too long, they all just looked at me as though I was speaking a foreign language, or something.

"And it's an actual job? Not just a hobby?" The Red-haired lady on the end asked.

"Nope. It's my job. I own my own business. I'm sorry. I didn't get your names."

"Jane."

"Jane."

"Jane."

All three of them commented, wiggled their fingers the same way the other woman had a few days before, and waited for my reply.

"Wait, so all of you are named Jane?"

They nodded.

"Wow! My name is---"

"Jane." They answered in unison.

"Yes. Mary Jane, actually. And the other lady that I met the other day, her name was Jane too."

"Yes."

Creepy! And I would be a fool to think that this was just a coincidence. No. It couldn't be.

"Just how many *Janes* are there around here?"

"Every woman, in every house, on our street."

"Really? Wow! I guess this street should be called "Jane Lane" instead, huh?" I chuckled but they didn't. I guess they missed the joke.

There was a strange silence and just as I opened my mouth to speak, one of the other Janes spoke instead.

"Well, if you ever need anything, don't hesitate to just knock on a door or two. Unlike you, the rest of us don't work, at least not in the traditional sense, so I'm sure one of us will be available to assist."

So, none of them had jobs or careers?

I guess this town was even more "out of date" than I thought.

Seeing Charity's truck pull into the driveway, instead of asking questions, I simply nodded.

"Thanks ladies, I'll keep that in mind."

Charity grabbed a few things and headed for the house, and the other ladies formed a line, and headed across the lawn in the other direction. They walked the same exact way as the other Jane walked a few days before; arms straight down by the sides---walk, skip, walk, skip.

They didn't speak to, acknowledge or even look in Charity's direction.

"New neighbors?"

"More like new Jane's," I commented.

"Huh?"

"All of their names are Jane."

"Wait, what? You're kidding."

"Nope. In fact, they said that every woman on this street is named Jane."

"Well, that's strange as hell, to say the least."

"Tell me about it. I wonder if the realtor knew this and why she hadn't mentioned it. It would've been a fun fact to know. Maybe that's why she'd added this house to our list of suggestions in the first place. Anyway, are you ready to get to work?"

She opened her purse.

"I got the booze."

"I got pie, and I'll get the cups," I laughed and headed for the kitchen.

After chatting and devouring pieces of the pie for a few minutes, we raised the windows, turned on the music and got to work. We both became consumed with the space and hours later, we high-fived, knowing that we'd worked our magic.

"Amazing!" I squealed as I eyed the yellow, mint, and grey color scheme that had come together so perfectly.

"Yeah it is. Thanks to me," Charity gloated.

"Whatever. I guess you are pretty good," I joked.

"Yeah. I am, aren't I? But you're better. You've always been better," Charity complimented me. "Uh oh, do you remember this song?" Charity eyes grew big and we both giggled in excitement.

It was one of our favorite songs from our college days. Some of the best memories of my life had been with Charity. We'd meet each other our freshman year of college, and were as close as two peas in a pod up to the time that we walked across the stage. After graduating, we remained friends, but of course life and our careers got in the way; especially on my end. I wanted success so bad, so I was always busy. Charity always found time to live while achieving in the process, but that had never been one of my many talents. Needless to say, after a while, hanging out with each other was a thing of the past. Eventually, the weekly calls and monthly e-mails stopped too.

And before we realized it, over three or four years had gone by, without us speaking to or hearing from each other. And then, over a year ago, we spotted each other at a convention and we've been stuck together like glue ever since.

We'd missed out on so many things and so much time. By the time we'd reconnected, she was divorced, and had a son. I'd just gotten married to Brice---with no maid of honor. But now that we were friends again, and business partners, life was just a little bit better with her around.

"Come on, show me that move you did that night on the table. Remember the party where Brice walked in, flipped out because you were drunk? He was so freaking mad that night, remember? And I was so drunk, that I couldn't help you. I just stood there and laughed," Charity laughed so hard that she started to choke. She then tried to mimic my old dance moves and I joined in with her to show her how it was done.

And then, abruptly, the radio in the kitchen stopped playing.

"What happened?"

"I don't know."

"I'll go check."

Charity disappeared into the kitchen, while I took pictures of the living room to send to Brice.

"Jane!"

I headed in Charity's direction.

She was holding up the cord to the radio. One end was in her hand and the other end was still in the socket. It looked as though the cord had been cut.

"Well, either you have a ghost who's scissor-happy, or a neighbor who doesn't like loud music," she said inspecting the cord as I looked around the backyard.

The backdoor was wide open but I was sure that it had been closed. Yet, no one was there. Everything was quiet.

I shook my head and after talking about the cord for a while longer, we called it a day and headed to the front porch to relax with wine and cheese.

"Do you really think someone cut that cord?"

"You saw the same cord that I saw. Someone definitely cut it. Unless somehow it popped into two pieces. But we would've heard that. Right? Well, the music was pretty loud, so maybe not. But then there would've been some kind of smoke or something. I think. Hell Jane, I'm drunk. I don't know."

Imagine how bold a person had to be to walk into someone's house and cut the cord on their radio!

Boy, I wished I'd caught them!

We watched some of the husbands walk into the different houses. All of them were wearing ties and black suits. I wondered if they all worked the same job, at the same place, since everything else seemed to be the same around here.

"Aside from whoever was being an ass, this neighborhood seems nice. It feels "homey" if you know what I mean. But it's too quiet for me though," Charity said. "Quiet neighborhoods are usually filled with a bunch of *crazies*," she laughed.

But I didn't. What if she was right?

Charity stayed for as long as she could, before having to leave to pick up her son. Soon after she was gone, Brice arrived.

He questioned me about my day and the work on the house as he approached the front porch.

"My day was interesting. Everything was fine and then all of a sudden---no music. And is looks like someone came through the back door and cut the power cord on the radio."

"Huh? That doesn't make any sense. Why would someone do that? Maybe it just popped or something."

I shrugged. "Yeah. I doubt it. And the back door was wide open. You know, more ladies from the neighborhood came by today and you'll never guess what their names were," I said to him as he took a seat on the porch swing beside me.

"No way. Are you kidding me?"

"Nope. All three of their names were Jane. As a matter of fact, the whole Lane is full of Jane's---one in every, single, house," I slurred. "The realtor had to have known this. I wonder why she didn't mention it. I don't know Brice, but something is weird. Something just doesn't feel right all of a sudden."

"Tell me about it. Well, we haven't sold the condo yet. We can always go back there and try to see if we can pull out of this in some way. I'll have Randy take a look at the paperwork and see what we can do," Brice said.

I sat for a while and thought about his words. Soon, I shook my head. "No. You don't have to do that. At least not yet. I really love this house. It's our dream home. And I wouldn't feel safe if we went back to the condo. But we need to keep our eyes open around here," I said, noticing that our next-door neighbor was staring at us out of her window.

She waved. I waved back.

She was one of the ladies that I hadn't spoken to as of yet but there was one thing that I already knew about her.

I already knew her name.

Jane.

~***********************~

CHAPTER TWO

All of the women were mowing their lawns; instead of the men. They were all riding the same type and color lawn mower, on the same day, at the same time, while wearing dresses, pearls and heels.

Weird.

As I drove by them, all of them stopped to wave.

I forced a smile and I continued down the road, glancing at them in my rearview mirror. Yes. Things in this neighborhood were definitely going to be interesting. But I tried to stay positive.

I followed the navigation system towards the small section of shopping centers of the town. I needed a few things to either start or complete a few house projects. It wasn't a huge selection of stores, but definitely a good variety. So, I prepared myself for a few hours of endless shopping.

I entered a furniture store, and surprisingly, I was greeted by name.

"Welcome Jane."

I looked at the store associate confused. I wasn't wearing a name tag or anything, so how did he know my name?

"Excuse me?"

"Is there anything in particular that you're looking for? I'll do my best to help."

"No. How did you know my name?"

"You are the new Jane in town…correct?"

"And how would you know that?"

"Everyone knows that."

He talked as though he didn't understand my confusion.

"But how would you know who I was?"

"It's on the bulletin board. In the breakroom. And we got an email. You are the new Jane. I memorized your face from the picture. I'm sure everyone around here has, so that we can properly greet you. "Janes" must be properly addressed."

"Picture! What do you mean a picture? Of me?"

"Yes. As a heads up of a new Jane."

Huh?

Freaked out and beyond confused, I left the cart right in front of him and turned to walk away. Suddenly, I wasn't in the mood to shop.

"Have a good day Jane," he yelled behind me, causing me to walk even faster in the opposite direction.

What the hell…

~***~

"Hi Jane," the Blonde Jane from across the street chimed. Since everyone had the same name and since I didn't know their last names, yet, I'd classified them by hair color, character traits or ethnicity.

"Hi!" I spoke, simply to be polite. I was still a little freaked out about what had happened at the store the other day. Brice suggested that I was overreacting and he assured me that the store, or any other store for that matter, didn't have a picture of me posted on their breakroom bulletin board. He assured me that it couldn't have possibly been true and we even went back to the store to see if I got the same reaction, but though the associates were friendly, no one called me by name. The gentleman that had been there earlier that day was gone, but I was positive that he'd called me by name. I even told Brice that he'd put emphases on my name calling me "A Jane", as though it meant something.

"I'm having a barbeque this weekend. Consider this your invite," she said with a guarantee. Hmm. A barbeque was the perfect place to ask a few questions. Maybe I could find out a little more about the area and about *The Janes*.

The ladies were weird, but they had been nothing but nice to me, so I agreed to come.

"Sure thing. We'll be there."

"Great. By the way, the lilies that you planted look nice but in case no one else told you, our neighborhood flower is the Perennials. As you can see, everyone has them. We took a vote. They're pretty and they really give our houses that extra pop, you know."

"Yeah. I noticed that. But I didn't like them, so I pulled them up and put the lilies down instead. I kind of have a thing for them---as you can tell," I said, pointing at the custom-made mailbox, I'd put up the day before. It was covered in white and yellow hand-painted lilies. I beamed at it, but Blonde Jane's smile disappeared. And she didn't bother to comment. She just waved goodbye, turned around and walked away.

I guess she doesn't like lilies.

I shrugged and just as I was about to get into my car I paused and looked at the house next door.

At this point, I'd met all of the Janes on our street; except for this one. She never came outside. And I never saw a husband go into her house either. I always caught her glancing out of her window, but for the most part, she wasn't as busy or as friendly as the others.

I'd nicknamed her Silent Jane.

I headed up her walk way, past the ugly little flowers and I knocked on the door and waited for her to open it.

I knew that she was home. She was always home.

"Hi neighbor, I'm Mary Jane, Jane for short."

She smiled.

Up close she was so much prettier than she appeared to be from the window. She had flawless peanut butter skin, and big, beautiful brown eyes. She was gorgeous. She too seemed to be slightly older than some of the rest of them.

"Hi. I'm..."

"Jane, of course," I answered for her and she nodded.

"So, I just wanted to say hello."

"Hello."

She waited for me to say something else. I looked past her. The layout to her home was identical to ours. And the living room was so clean that you could eat right off the floor. Everything was cleaned to perfection; except for her hands. Little red spots were all over them.

Maybe she was making one of those cherry pies.

She noticed my gaze, but she didn't say a word.

"Well, as I said, I just wanted to introduce myself and officially meet you. I guess you'll be at the barbeque at the Blonde Jane's house this weekend."

"Blonde Jane?"

I hadn't meant to say my little nick name aloud, so I pointed to the house.

"Jane Peterson. Yes. I'll see you there," she said and once she placed her hand on the door knob, I took that as my signal to leave. And so I did. She shut the door before I'd even walked down the first step.

As I walked back towards my car, I heard children laughing again and I turned around to see if I could spot them. I always heard them, but to date, I had never actually seen a single child on our street; not one. And I couldn't help but wonder why.

I glanced back to catch Silent Jane looking out of her window---again. She didn't move once I saw her. She just stood there and stared at me until I drove away.

There was something up with the Janes on S.J. Lane, and I was sure that they wouldn't be able to hide it forever.

~***~

"Are you asleep?"

"No. Actually, I'm headed back home. Brice isn't feeling well, so I had to find a 24-hour drugstore to get him some medicine. What are you doing up so late?" I asked Charity, as I turned onto my street. It was after midnight, and I for one, couldn't wait to curl up in bed.

"I was looking over a few things for the Emerald Hotel lobby project. I think I found a scheme that works better. I just can't remember the password to access that new design program you installed."

"JNC2017," I commented just as I pulled into our driveway.

"Okay, I'm in. I'll show you what I've been working on tomorrow. Good night," she said, and hung up her phone. I turned off the car and gathered my things.

Once I opened the car door, I paused.

Someone was yelling. It sounded like an argument. I couldn't tell what they were saying, but I could hear them shouting. It sounded as though it was coming from the house on the corner, but I couldn't be sure.

I was surprised. The neighborhood was always so quiet and pleasant during the day that a midnight spat just didn't seem normal. It didn't seem to fit.

But minding my business, I grabbed my bags, got out of my car and I headed inside.

Minutes later, after clearing out the bags and fumbling through my purse, I noticed that I didn't have my cell phone. I'd probably sat it in the passenger seat after hanging up with Charity. Brice called my name but I told him that I was going back out to the car to see if I'd left my phone in there.

I slipped back on my shoes and opened the front door.

"Boo!" Blonde Jane screamed and popped up as though she'd been squatting down by the front door.

"Ahh!" I yelled and before I could stop myself, I punched her.

Immediately I covered my mouth, but she just giggled, loudly, as she rubbed her forehead.

"Jane!" I heard Brice yell and then I heard his footsteps.

"I'm okay!" I yelled and then I started to yell at her. "What the hell are you doing? You almost gave me a heart attack!"

Blonde Jane continued to laugh and handed me my keys that I'd dropped out of fright. "I saw you get out of the car. I was coming up the street and I saw that you left your car light on. I was coming to tell you but just before I knocked, I heard your keys and heard you opening the door. So, I thought it would be fun to give you a little scare." She snickered as I glanced at the car. The light inside of my car was on. But I wasn't sure how.

Brice appeared at the top of the stairs.

"You should've just knocked on the door! You scared the hell out of me!" I chastised her as I turned on the porch light, and closed the front door behind me.

What crazy person tries to scare someone at this time of night?

"Sorry," she said following me to my car.

I opened the car door, and found my phone, which was actually in the cup holder. I pressed the button to turn off the light, even though I was sure that I'd never turned it on.

Blonde Jane just stood there.

I found it weird that she was still fully dressed at midnight. I wondered if that had been her, arguing with someone only moments before.

I noticed that she had little red spots all over her dress; identical to the ones that were on Silent Jane's hands the other day.

"Was that you that I heard yelling a little while ago?"

"What did you hear?" She asked. She stood in the same spot as I walked towards the porch.

"I didn't hear anything specific, just yelling. It was coming from somewhere down the street," I eyed the spots on her dress again and she followed my gaze.

"It was probably me giving Jane Jordan an earful. I'm trying to teach her to make my famous cherry pie but what can I say…she's a slow learner."

"Baking a pie? At midnight?"

"We bake all the time around here. We're up late most nights too. We're night people. You'll see," she said as I shrugged. I glanced at her dress again. I guess the spots could be from the cherries.

"Well, goodnight," I said to her.

"Good night, Jane."

Still, she stood in the same spot as I walked inside and as I shut the door behind me.

Curious, I peered secretly out of the blinds at her. She walked and skipped, speedily across the street towards her house. I walked away from the window, but I had the sudden urge to look back out of it again and when I did, I saw Blonde Jane make a U-turn at her front door, and skip down the street, in the same direction that the yelling had been coming from. From that window, I couldn't see which house she'd gone into, but I was no fool. Wherever she was going, whatever she was doing, didn't have a damn thing to do with baking a cherry pie! And I was sure about that.

~***~

"Brice, did you pull up our flowers?"

I'd gone into the office that day, and when I arrived home, the lilies that I'd planted were gone. Every single one of them had been replaced by the ugly white and fuchsia neighborhood flower, the Perennials.

"What? No. Why would I do that? What's wrong?"

I didn't answer his question. I was too busy looking at the mailbox. My custom-made mailbox with the white and yellow lilies was nowhere in sight. Instead, the mailbox that had been there when we moved in, had replaced it.

"Someone changed our mailbox."

"What do you mean?"

"Nothing. I'll see you when you get home," I said, as I stared at the Blonde Jane getting out of her car. She turned and waved at me. She waited for me to wave back but instead, I walked towards her.

"Hello Jane," she said first.

"Hi. I was wondering, have you seen anyone around my house today?"

"No, I haven't. I'm sorry. I've been running errands all day. Is something wrong?"

She was grinning at me pleasantly and I couldn't tell if her smile was genuine or if she was only smiling out of habit.

"Um, no. Nothing is wrong," I lied.

“Okay, well, I have to get in to start prepping for tomorrow’s barbeque. See you tomorrow,” she said, heading towards her front door. “Oh, by the way Jane, I love the changes that you’ve made over there. I’m glad you got rid of those lilies. The Perennials look so much better,” she said, just before closing her front door.

With a confused look on my face, slowly, I walked back across the street towards my house.

Seeing Silent Jane step onto her porch to shake a rug, I knew that she’d been home all day, she never went anywhere, but I figured that she probably wouldn’t tell me even if she had seen something or someone messing around my yard. She never spoke to me. Always waved, always smiled, but never said a word.

I stood there, looking at my yard, still in disbelief.

First the radio incident, and now this? Apparently, someone in this neighborhood didn’t understand the meaning of personal property and boundaries.

Someone was asking for me to trade in my 6-inch pumps, for a pair of tennis shoes and *Vaseline*. And I was sure that this neighborhood wasn’t ready for that type of Jane.

Speaking of, I took off my shoes, headed to get the shovel and then I started to dig up the flowers that had been planted without my permission. This is my house. My yard. And I was going to have the flowers that I wanted.

It took a while but just as the sun started to go down, I placed the bag of the Perennials on the side of the road as trash. I was hot and sweaty, but I was making a point. I looked around, but no one was there. No one was watching, well, at least not where I could see them.

But hopefully the message was clear.

We all may have the same name, but this Jane has her own style, and her own brain. I liked to be different and whoever didn't like it, was just going to have to get used to it. Because I wouldn't be bullied into blending in.

"What happened to the yard?" Brice asked me the next morning.

"I told you, somebody pulled up my lilies and replanted those ugly ass flowers that's in everyone else's yard. So, I pulled them up. I'll plant more lilies when I get the time. Can you believe that someone would do that? And they changed our damn mailbox!"

"No, but I'm going to get to the bottom of it."

"You and me both."

"Now come here and give me some *sugar*," Brice poked out his lips.

"I have a feeling that the Blonde Jane across the street had something to do with it. I don't know why. It's just a feeling. What time did you get home last night?"

"It was late. I had a project that I wanted to finish up before I left. When I got in, you were already asleep," Brice said, and he kissed me since I hadn't made a move to kiss him like he'd asked.

"Do you even want to go to this barbeque?"

"We don't have to. We can stay in all day and be nasty. I like that idea way better. I mean like *wayyyyy* better," he said as though he was mimicking something that I would say. He reached for my hands and then forced me to stand to my feet.

"I don't know, maybe we should. You haven't actually met anyone yet and I want you to see what I'm saying about these women. They're strange Brice. It's just something about them. Something I'm not seeing," I said to Brice, who was more focused on my breasts.

"Okay, we will go, but it the meantime…"

Brice took off his shirt. His 6-foot frame glowed from the morning sun. Brice wasn't what most would call attractive, but he oozed with sex appeal. His skin was smooth and creamy, like buttermilk. He was a lighter complexion, since he was part African American and part

Irish. His hair was short and only a shade or two darker than red and his brown eyes were mesmerizing. His big nose and crocked smile had grown on me over the years and there wasn't a stitch of fat on his body. Something about him was just sort of erotic but the best part about him was that he was all mine.

"Arms up," he said as I raised my arms above my head so that he could remove my night gown.

He eyed my naked frame as if he'd hit the jackpot or something. Now I, unlike Brice, was all out of shape. I wasn't plus size, but I wasn't skinny either. My breasts were full, my thighs rubbed together, and I had a small little pouch that I assumed came from drinking too much. I was barely five feet tall and the same exact color as chocolate, with a head full of curly black hair.

"Is it time to start making babies yet?" Brice asked as he pushed me up against our bedroom window.

"Humph, I've been ready. I was waiting on you," I smirked and switched positions with him.

I kissed his ears and his neck, as he cooed. I made my way down to his nipples and as I flicked the left one with my tongue, I placed my index finger in his mouth and moaned once he started to suck it. After a while, I made my way down to his boxers and got comfortable on my knees. I glanced up at him. His eyes were closed and as always, his manhood was standing at attention. I prepared my mouth to devour his main missile but for some reason, I glanced beside of him, out of the window.

And never the less, two Janes were standing there, staring up at our bedroom window, watching us.

"Oh Shit!"

I moved and Brice jumped.

"What?"

"Close the blinds!"

He frowned and turned around to close them.

"What?"

"They saw us."

"Who?"

I crawled back over to the window and peeked out of it but no one was there.

"Nothing," I said as Brice pulled me towards the bed.

Later that evening, as promised, we headed across the street for the barbeque.

As soon as we entered the backyard, Blonde Jane headed in our direction. Surprisingly, everything and everyone looked normal. The women were either in dresses or bikinis and the men were dressed casually as well. It didn't look like some kind of ritual or something, which in a weird way, I was somewhat expecting.

"Hi neighbors! Thanks for coming," she roared and I reached her the cake that I'd bought from the store. Her breath smelled like she'd just eaten a diaper full of baby's shit but I managed to keep a straight face and forced my lips to keep smiling. Briefly, I glanced at Brice who was also fake smiling, but I could tell that he was holding his breath.

"Aww, Jane, you shouldn't have. Thank you," she squealed. "Nice to finally meet you Brice. Now run along! The men have been waiting for you. We will take good care of *your* Jane." Brice damn near ran in the other direction. She nodded for me to follow her towards a few of the other ladies.

"I'm going to sit this in the kitchen. I'll be right back," she bellowed. I finally exhaled once she walked away. As I inhaled the fresh air, I glanced at the table of deserts and wondered why she hadn't placed the cake there. But then again, it wouldn't have been any room for it since the table was filled with way too many cherry pies.

What is it about these pies?

"So, how are things so far? Are you enjoying your new house?" The Red-haired Jane asked.

“Yes, for the most part. But something weird has been going on with my flowers and my mailbox is missing. Have any of you seen anything?”

The ladies shook their heads no.

“Well, I did see something that I wasn’t supposed to see,” a voice said from behind me. It was one of the Janes that had been watching me and Brice that morning from the street. She was mixed; I assumed part Caucasian and part Black. She wasn’t all that attractive and it was something about her nose that made her look sort of wicked.

“Taking my morning walks just got a little bit better,” she laughed.

“I’m so sorry about that. I’m so embarrassed. Brice has this crazy ritual of opening the curtains and blinds as soon as he’s out of the bed so that the sunlight can shine through. And we somewhat forgot and…”

“Oh, no need to apologize. I hadn’t had sex with my husband in about four months---well, until this morning,” she blushed. Everyone else either giggled or made naughty comments. Blonde Jane smiled as she approached the conversation.

“What did I miss?”

“Somebody gave us a little show this morning,” giggled the Jane standing next to me. And the conversation started up again.

“Oh, nothing is wrong with some spare of the moment sex. How many months had it been?” Blonde Jane asked.

“For what?”

“Sex,” she said as if I was stupid.

“What do you mean months? We have sex almost every day. Twice a day, if I’m lucky,” I winked at her.

“And he actually wants to?” Red-haired Jane asked as the Latino one elbowed her.

“Hell yeah. All the time,” I smiled but everyone else looked at me with a scowl.

“Well, I guess, we married the wrong men, huh ladies,” Blonde Jane broke the ice, and laughter and chatter started up again.

I glanced at Brice. He was smoking a cigar and holding a drink. The men appeared to be talking to him all at once. He was simply nodding. The sight of him made me smile.

I’d wanted this for us. A neighborhood full of people, married people, that we could become friends with. But I though this moment was perfect, this particular neighborhood might not be so perfect for us after all.

I looked around the yard. Two of the Janes were splashing each other in the pool. A few of the others were drinking and eating. And then there was the group right near me that was still chatting. But I noticed that something was missing.

"Where are the children?"

"Children aren't allowed at barbeques."

"Why?"

"It's just the way that we do things around here. It gives the parents a little time to bond without responsibilities," Blonde Jane said. Surprisingly, the other women nodded, confirming that they agreed. It was one of the stupidest things I'd ever heard but I was quickly learning that there were far too many rules and untraditional practices amongst this group.

"I guess there are a lot of rules around here, huh?"

No one answered my question. They just continued talking as though they hadn't heard it. So, I didn't say anything else. I stood by, silently, and just watched them.

I listened to the way that they talked and I watched their body language. Their conversation was normal. Nothing strange jumped out at me. They talked very proper; as though they were very well educated, yet none of them chose to work. I also noticed that none of them cursed. Not even once.

My focus and everyone else's shifted to Silent Jane coming around the corner.

"Doesn't she look pretty?" One of the Janes whispered behind me. "Doesn't she always? I'm surprised she hasn't found herself a new husband yet," another Jane answered her.

A new husband? Okay. So, she must be divorced.

That explained why I never saw a husband go in or out of her house.

Everyone greeted her except for me. I just looked on at the interaction. Silent Jane babbled away, which surprised me. She'd been a woman of very few words, but in that moment, she talked restlessly. Maybe it was just that she hadn't wanted to talk to me.

I found myself mesmerized by her beauty but catching the look on some of the other Janes faces, instead of awe, I saw jealousy and envy. She wiggled her fingers at me as I headed for the table loaded with alcohol.

I was going to need a few drinks to get through this evening and after about five shots of vodka, I relaxed and eventually, I started to enjoy myself.

They had drinking games, good food, and plenty of chatting and conversation. But I noticed that there was no music or dancing. Another thing that I noticed was that the men never blended with the women. The husbands stayed on one side and the wives stayed on the other. The women didn't even fix their husband's plate. And whenever Brice and I would meet up to talk for a second or to kiss, they would pull us both back in different directions.

Weird.

"Can I use the restroom?"

"Sure. Our houses are made the same, so you know where it is," Blonde Jane said as she took another drink.

I headed inside. I observed her house on the way to the bathroom. It was simple and basic. I definitely wouldn't have used the decorator that she'd tried to suggest.

The house was clean as a whistle, just like Silent Jane's and it smelled good too. The walls were bare. No decorations. No art or store-bought pictures. Nor were there any family pictures, not even a wedding photo.

I entered the bathroom. It matched the vibe of the rest of the house. Once I was done, I checked the medicine cabinet. Nothing out of the ordinary. No crazy people medicine or anything. I looked in the linen closet and even moved the shower curtain to check the tub. Everything looked normal.

I took a deep breath. But something was still off about them, especially this Blonde One.

I headed back through the kitchen and just as I turned the knob on the back door, I noticed the cake that I'd brought to the barbeque. It was in the trash. I touched the container. It had a butcher's knife stabbed through it, right in the center of the cake.

See. I knew it! This bitch is crazy!

I was stuck for a few moments, but I forced my feet to move, placed on a smile and headed back outside, where they all appeared to be waiting for me.

I managed to fake my way through the rest of the night and finally it was time to leave. Everyone headed out at the same time. The Janes and their husbands went in separate directions as Brice and I took a seat on the front porch swing. After a few moments, all was quiet.

"Brice, these people…"

"Are nutcases."

I looked at him.

"Even the men?"

"I mean, they were okay. But none of them like their wives."

"What? What do you mean?"

"Just what I said. They talked about them most of them time. And not in a good way. They talked about them having crazy rules and most of them are having affairs."

"Really?"

"Yep."

"That explains why they don't have sex for months at a time. The women thought that it was strange that you and I have sex all the time."

"It's strange that they don't."

I nodded.

"Oh, and you and Silent Jane are the only Janes that didn't grow up with the others. The rest of them have known each other for years. Silent Jane moved in a few years ago. Her husband died not long after moving here and they said that they're wives were always on her about finding a new one."

Wow. I guess that's why they were all so much alike. Even Silent Jane had fallen in line with their looks and their ways. And she wasn't divorced. She was a widow.

"The Blonde Jane's husband said that she's a real bitch and a control freak."

"And they told you all of this?"

“They were sloppy drunk. They would’ve told me their checking account numbers had I asked for them. But I didn’t have to ask anything. They spoke of the Janes and their affairs all on their own. But I got the feeling that they are all staying with their wives because they feel like they have to; not because they want to. As though they are afraid of them. And I’m pretty sure that they are hiding something. It was like a secret hanging over us, that none of them were bold enough to share.

I sat in deep thought, and Brice was quiet for a while too. And then finally he spoke again.

“I don’t know, but what do you say about giving our lawyer, Randy, a call in the morning? Maybe we can find some options, or maybe try to work out something with the seller. I mean, it hasn’t been that long. And if we have to put the house right back on the market, I’m okay with that too. I just don’t think that we are a good fit for this neighborhood, you know.”

I exhaled loudly. “I know I don’t say this often, but I think you might be right,” I laughed and Brice did too, but we both knew that we were serious.

~***~

The Janes were gathered together on Blonde Jane’s front porch. It was early in the morning but there they were, fully dressed, having some kind of meeting or something. I saw Blonde Jane point to each of them as though she was designating them with a task and the Jane that she pointed to would simply nod her head.

I finished getting dressed for work and by the time I came back to the window, they were all gone.

"Guess who sold us this house?" Brice said scrolling on his phone.

"Who?"

"Jane Peterson."

"Blonde Jane?"

"Yep. She was its first and only owner, before us. And the house was only in her name. Her husband's name wasn't listed."

"So, they put the house up for sale and moved across the street? But why? The houses are exactly the same."

"I don't know. But Randy looked over the paperwork. Basically, the only choice we have is to resell it. Put it right back on the market. I mean the price was so good that we bought it in cash. So, we don't have to worry about a loan issues. That's a good thing."

"Why didn't we know that they she was the seller before?"

"I don't remember the realtor ever calling her name; at least not her first name. But it's there in black and white. We acted on it so quickly, I guess the names of the owners hadn't been a big deal. The price was right and we wanted to hop on it as fast as we could; and not to mention that we were in such a hurry to get out of the condo, because of the break-in. Remember?"

I nodded.

We spoke a little more about the house and then Brice rushed off to work. A few minutes after, I headed out the door, but I had a few minutes to spare, so I headed over to Blonde Jane's house.

Blonde Jane was the one that I was worried about the most. She was the weirdest. She was the leader; the other Janes followed. I could see us having some major issues and problems in the future, if we stayed here.

I knocked a few times before she finally came to the door.

"Good morning, I wanted to talk to you about something."

"Sure."

"You were the previous owner of our house."

"That's right."

"What made you move out of it?"

"I liked this view of the street better. Is everything okay?"

"Yes. Brice and I are just thinking about putting the house back on the market. It's not that we don't love the house…"

"Then what is it?"

"Well," I took a second to think of a lie. "Brice just got a new project at work. Longer hours and the project will last for quite some time. We still haven't sold our condo and we just think that it's probably best to move back, closer to his job." Hell, I could've come up with a better lie than that.

For a couple of seconds, she was strangely quiet, and then she spoke.

"You're tired of us already Jane?"

"No. Of course not. It's for work purposes."

She didn't reply.

"Well, I was just wondering. I have to get to work," I said to her.

"Okay. But, just so you know, we're very, what's the word, "selective" around here. What I'm trying to say is that usually, in this community, once we let you in…you stay in. Well, unless you die or something. Anyway, enjoy your day Jane!" She waved and laughed loudly, as I walked away.

What did she mean by that?

Once at work, I filled Charity in on The Janes.

She suggested that we simply go back to the condo until we figured things out.

"Is it really that bad?"

"Charity, I just don't know what it is. I can't put my finger on it but it's something weird about them."

"Um, well, I think I believe you," Charity nodded towards the glass window.

We both stared at Blonde Jane and two other Janes, as they waved and smiled at me from the office window.

"What the…"

They kept waving, as though they were waiting on me to wave back at them. But I didn't. Instead, Charity waved. Instantly, they stopped waving and walked away.

"See. I told you," I frowned. "And how did they know where I worked? I told them what I did, but I never told them where I worked."

"Maybe they just really like you."

"Or maybe they're just really crazy!" I pouted.

For the rest of the day, I had to listen to Charity and her hundreds of reasons why we needed to get the hell out of that house. And though I absolutely agreed with her, hours later, dreadfully, I headed towards S.J. Lane.

I pulled up at home, to see that the neighborhood flower, the Perennials, had been neatly replanted in our yard…again!

"Un-freaking-believable!" I groaned, rolled my eyes and stepped on as many of them as I could, on my way to check the mailbox.

I spotted two Janes, walking one dog; and I mean literally, both Janes had their hands on one leash, walking the same damn dog!

"Seriously?" I mumbled in a disturbed confusion.

Both Janes waved at me with their free hand, but I didn't wave back. The sight of them just confirmed what I already knew.

The sooner that we sold this house…

The better.

~***************************~

CHAPTER THREE

"Ummm," I moaned as Brice gave me the *business* from behind. I gripped the sheets tighter and tighter as Brice talked dirty to me. But just as I was about to reply, we heard something shatter.

Instantly, we both froze. I looked back at Brice who appeared to be listening.

"What was that?"

"I don't know. Don't worry about it," he answered and slowly started to stroke again.

"No, Brice. No. Go see."

He pouted and after I repeated myself, he stopped and headed towards the bedroom door. Naked and breathless, I followed him and stood at the top of the stairs to wait for him. After a few minutes, he came back, holding pieces of a vase. And not just any ole' vase. It was the vase that I'd intentionally placed behind the back door.

Whether it was when I arrived home from work or just random times throughout the day, somehow, I always found our backdoor wide open. Even if I was certain that I'd shut and locked it, it was always open. And that meant that someone from the outside was coming in.

So, I came up with the idea to booby-trap it. I'd placed a vase on a small stand, right up against the door, so that if the door opened, from the outside, it wouldn't have a choice but to knock it over.

"I told you! I told you that someone is coming in here! I told you!"

Brice looked at the broken pieces that he was holding and then back at me. He didn't say anything, he just disappeared for a while and I waited at the top of the stairs.

"The back door was unlocked," he said once he reappeared and headed up the stairs for him.

It couldn't be anymore clearer if it hit us in our face. This house wasn't going to work for us, no matter how much we loved it and no matter what little part of us wanted to stay.

Later that evening, I sat on the front porch and enjoyed to cool breeze. I smiled as Silent Jane appeared on her front porch and took a seat.

"Hey Jane," I yelled to her but she didn't respond. She just sat there as though I hadn't said a thing.

"It feels good out here, doesn't it? Do you want some company? Maybe we can sit and chat for a while," I suggested. But still she, she said nothing and a few seconds later, she got up, and silently went on her way.

~***~

The condo was sold, and our next focus was putting the house up for sell. We hadn't had anymore backdoor incidents, since we'd changed the locks, but I still didn't feel safe---or maybe it was that I didn't feel comfortable. Either way, it was just too much, too soon, and we still wanted out.

Brice and I both decided to take the day off, just to ride around and look for rental properties in neighboring towns. After a few hours, we headed back home.

"Maybe you should do some things around the house and yard. There are a few things that you've been putting off. After all, we are about to try and sell," I said to Brice. The house was in good shape, but there were a few things in the house and yard that needed a little extra attention.

He agreed, and while he changed into something comfortable, I decided to put on my swimsuit and enjoy the pool. I might as well get at least one swim out of it and since I didn't feel safe enough to swim if Brice wasn't home, this might be my only chance.

Brice got started in the yard and with a glass of champagne, I pressed play on my music playlist on my phone, connected it to my wireless headphones, placed on my shades and then I entered the pool and sat on the float.

"Yes," I exhaled. I was convinced that once we found a new house, it had to have a pool. The music relaxed me, as the warmth of the sun kissed my skin, I was reminded that we were well overdue for a vacation. Completely relaxed for the first time in weeks, I closed my eyes. But that didn't last long. The ringing in my ears, from the incoming call on my phone, interrupted my music. I groaned and opened my eyes. And…

"Hey Jane."

I screamed and went tumbling into the water.

Blonde Jane had been standing there, in our pool, right beside my float. I came up from under the water and saw her still standing there, with the pool water up to her chest, simply smiling at me.

"What the hell are you doing in here?"

I screamed at her as I wiped the water from my eyes.

"We wanted to invite you to dinner."

"And you had to get in my pool to ask me that?"

She didn't respond.

"Get the hell out of the pool!" I yelled at her as I too, headed towards the edge of the pool. She floated towards the pool's steps and I watched her as she got out of the water. She was fully dressed. She'd even kept on her shoes.

Her dress was soaked, dripping as she waited on my answer.

"Don't you ever bring your ass over here again! Do you understand me?"

"Is that a no on dinner?" She inquired.

"It's a hell no! What is wrong with you? You can't just come over to people's house, uninvited, and get into their pool! You can't force yourself into someone's life! You can't force yourself into their space! Or into their house! Get out the hell out of my backyard! Now!"

Even though her eyes told me that she was upset by my response, she continued to smile the entire time and finally without saying a word, soak and wet she walked away.

"Brice!!!!"

~***~

"Wake up," Charity tapped me on the shoulder.

"I'm up. I'm sorry. I'm just so tired. I can't sleep at night in that house," I complained.

Though the Janes had been quiet lately, and still their happy, usual selves, I was always on edge. I always found myself watching them. Spying on them from the windows. Brice had started to say that I was obsessed with them, and I was starting to think that he might be right.

But I felt the need to always be alert. I felt that I always had to be on my toes and I didn't know how much longer I could live like that.

"Just stay to yourself until you find something."

"I've tried that. It doesn't work. And no matter how much I curse at them or decline their invites, they come by my house to invite me anyway. I guess they are hoping that one day, I'll change my mind. But I won't. I don't want anything to do with any of them. I just want them to leave me alone."

My eyes were heavy and at the end of my sentence, I closed them.

"Jane. I can handle things here. Just go home and get some sleep."

"That will never happen."

"Well, here, take my keys and go by my house and get a nap."

I shook my head. "Too far."

"You need sleep. Go to the back and take a nap then."

I shook my head.

"Jane, you're not going to work at your full potential like this. Listen to me. Go get some rest."

She was right. And ten minutes later, I was home, and lying on the couch. Surprisingly, I was too tired to worry about the Janes and within seconds, I was fast asleep.

A few hours later, refreshed, I headed towards the kitchen to make a sandwich but I paused just as I passed by the front door.

I watched the door knob turn slowly. I waited to see what was next and finally the knob was released and there was a knock.

"Jane. It's me," Blonde Jane said.

Of course, it was. I especially didn't want to talk to her, but out of curiosity, I opened the door anyway.

"Hello Jane. My family owns a boat. This weekend, we are taking a little ride. Just the ladies. We would love for you to join us."

"No, thanks. I have plans with my husband this weekend," I lied, since the normal "no" didn't seem to faze her.

"Jane, correct me if I'm wrong, but I'm starting to get the feeling that you don't like us very much," Blonde Jane said and I noticed that there were two other Janes standing at the bottom of my porch steps. Both of them frowned.

"I would just rather spend my free time with my husband."

"But why?"

"Why, what? That's what married people do." I would be the first to say that their views on marriage sucked! I could see why their husbands cheated on them.

"What if he doesn't have time spend with you? Then would you be available to come? Who knows, he may get busy at work or something. You never know."

"Trust me, he will have time. I'm his top priority."

"Says who?"

"Excuse me?"

"I mean, you just seem so sure, is all," she speculated.

"And I am. You know, I'm sorry that your husbands don't really like you, but mine is actually quite fond of me," I barked at all of them. Immediately, I bit my bottom lip.

It was definitely none of my business, nor my place, to repeat what Brice had told me, but they, the Blonde Jane, especially, was on my last nerve! She was always in my space, always in my face, and I just wanted her to go away!

I didn't say anything else and neither did she as I shut the door in her face. I made sure that it was locked and continued to the kitchen to fix myself something to eat. Once I was comfortable on the couch, with my food, I opened the blinds so that I could watch them.

"What the hell----"

Blonde Jane was on her knees, on my porch, right in front of the window.

"This bitch right here," I mumbled as she put a phone to her ear and grinned at me as mine started to ring.

"Hello?"

"Jane."

"How did you get my number?"

"We all have your number Jane. Anyway, I think that we should have a little chat."

I didn't respond.

"Forgive us if we've made a bad first impression, but that wasn't our intentions. But here's a thought: You would be much happier in this house, in this neighborhood, if you would just get onboard with the way that things are done around here."

"And how is that exactly?"

"Our way. The Janes way. Let me let you in on a little secret, this community, this town---is ours. We allowed you in, so in a way, you should feel special. Anything you want, anything you need, all you have to do is ask. You're a Jane honey. That carries a lot of weight around here. We welcomed you into our circle, but we are starting to feel a little rejected."

"Well, I don't want to be a part of your little circle. So, don't try to include me. See, that was easy. Problem solved."

"We want to be your friend Jane. You would hate to be our enemy. If I were you, I would get with the program darling. Okay? Think about our invitation again. Hopefully you'll change your mind. If I were you, I would," she exhaled loudly and then simply hung up.

I looked at her out of the window.

Did she just threaten me?

She got up off of her knees without taking her eyes off of me until it was time for her to walk down the front steps.

Immediately I called Brice, but he didn't answer, but checking the time, he should have surely been on his way home anyway.

Blonde Jane was a lunatic and I wondered if I could convince Brice to stay in a hotel until we found a rental house.

Finally, Brice pulled into the driveway and I met him at the front door.

"Baby, let's celebrate!" He walked in smiling, holding champagne.

"Celebrate?"

“I, well my company, scored big today. We got a new client, who just happens to own one of the largest companies on the East Coast. He hired us to do some huge projects for him. We’ll be starting immediately!” Brice was so happy and I didn’t want to ruin the moment with talks of moving and of The Janes.

“Congratulations baby,” I said instead.

“Thank you. This is major Jane! It really is! I already have so many ideas! I’ll be up late tonight, putting some things together. And I’ll probably be going in to the office this weekend too,” he said. At his comment, I couldn’t help but think of Blonde Jane’s comments from earlier that day.

Had she somehow sent this new client his way?

To keep him busy this weekend on purpose?

“And, babe, I was thinking, since I’m going to be working, a lot, to make these deadlines, I know that we were trying to figure out how, or when we were going to move, but can we just wait for a while? I just need to focus. I’m going to get an alarm system for the house, the good kind, with video monitoring and recording. And as long as we stay to ourselves, I think we should be fine. Just for a little while. Two or three months, at the most. You understand, don’t you?”

Hell no! But I dared not say my thoughts aloud. I nodded instead. Now wasn't the time to tell him how I really felt. But I didn't care if I had to find the house, sign the paperwork, and have our things moved, all on my own---that's just what I would have to do.

Brice kissed my lips and then he headed upstairs as I headed towards my phone. There was a new text message from an unsaved number waiting for me. I read it aloud, knowing that it was from Blonde Jane.

"I'm almost certain that you will be free this weekend! I'll save you a spot on the boat! Chao!"

"Like hell you will," I mumbled. "Like hell you will."

~***~

"Hey, I remember you," I said to the woman pumping her gas.

"No. I'm sorry. You must have me confused with someone else," she said.

"No. You're the woman who gave me the realtor's card. Remember? That morning at the coffee shop."

She screwed on her gas cap, but she didn't respond.

"You live around here? In Smithfield? What were you doing in Raleigh getting coffee? Oh. You must work somewhere around there huh?" I quizzed her, but she ignored me, and opened her car door.

What is up with the people in this town?

I was sure that it was her. And I got the feeling that she was trying to pretend as though she didn't remember me for a reason. So, I acted quickly. Before she could close her door, I grabbed it.

"You gave me the card to the realtor. At the coffee shop. Remember?"

She exhaled and looked around.

"Look lady. All I know is that a woman stopped me and asked me if I wanted to make $100. I go to school in Raleigh; I'm in medical school. She just tapped me on the shoulder and asked me to go into the coffee shop and somehow get you the card. I was just going to sneak it into your purse, but just so happens, you mentioned something about finding a house on the phone, creating the perfect opportunity to present the card to you."

What was she talking about?

"Who was this woman?"

"I don't know. She said that she was a realtor."

"What did she look like?"

"Honestly, I can't remember. I needed the $100, so I didn't ask any questions."

It just didn't make sense. Why would the realtor pay someone to give me her card, instead of just walking up and giving it to me herself? And how could she have known that I was looking for a house in the first place?

"Can I go now?"

I didn't answer her. I just let go of her car door.

She slammed it shut and drove away.

My thoughts were all over the place.

Once I was inside of my car, I grabbed my phone and tapped on the realtor's number. We hadn't seen, spoken to, or heard from her since the paperwork was signed and everything was final, but I was sure that she wouldn't mind answering a few questions.

I waited for the phone to ring but it didn't.

"The number you have reached is no longer in service. Please check the number and try your call again later."

What?

I typed the address from the business card into my GPS. Following the directions on the navigation system, I talked to myself aloud all the way there. Something was definitely fishy about all of this. And I wasn't surprised to pull up to an abandoned office building with a "For Rent" sign in the window.

All of a sudden, the house, The Janes, everything felt like some kind of set up. I could only assume that the realtor, or whoever gave her the card to give to me, never intended on me running into the woman again.

I wasn't supposed to know that she'd been paid to send me in the realtor's direction. Somebody was up to something. I recalled Blonde Jane's comments saying that they "let" me in.

Let me in what exactly?

I wasn't sure. But I was certain that someone wanted me to buy that house. Someone wanted me to meet the Janes.

But why?

~***~

I rolled out of bed and headed towards the bathroom. For the past two days, I'd been feeling awful.

"Brice!"

I yelled for him and when he didn't answer, I headed back into the bedroom to find my phone. He'd left a text, telling me that he'd gone in to work early and that he'd driven my car since I'd blocked him in.

I headed to look out the window. Indeed, my car was gone but quickly I turned my attention to Blonde Jane across the street.

She'd gotten out of her car and headed towards her trunk. She looked from side to side and then behind her. I let the blinds shut and stepped back. Hopefully she hadn't seen me. A few seconds later, I peeked out of them again. The trunk was open and she appeared to be looking for something.

Wait…what is that?

I inched closer to the window, closed my eyes and then looked again. Blonde Jane was looking for something and just as she was about to close the trunk, an arm came out of it. Hurriedly, she pushed it back inside.

I gasped and let go of the blinds.

"Oh, my God! Oh, my God!"

My hands started to shake and I tried to steady my heartbeat as I sat on the edge of the bed.

There was somebody in her trunk!

I grabbed my phone, dialed 911 and glanced back outside. Blonde Jane was headed into her house.

"911. What's your emergency?"

I tried to get my thoughts together before I spoke.

"Yes. I, uh, I was calling because I saw someone put a body in their trunk." The operator asked questions, giving me more time to think of what I wanted to say. "Uh, I don't know who is in the trunk. But they are in there. I followed the car to a house. I have the address if you are ready."

I gave them Blonde Jane's address and the operator assured me that help was on the way.

I stood there in shock, waiting to see what happened next. I'd known that she was strange and maybe even a little crazy, but just how crazy was she?

With the sudden urge to vomit, I forced myself to stop watching and ran to the bathroom. I was gone for all of two minutes and when I returned to the window, two police cars were pulling up in front of Blonde Jane's house. One of them headed towards her front door and the other one stood by her car.

I held my breath as I watched her step outside and talk to the officer. As always, she wore a smile. The officer followed her into the house and soon they came back outside with Blonde Jane and carrying her car keys.

My heart stopped beating as they opened the trunk. Both officers leaned over to look around inside of it. I watched them pull a few things out, here and there, but they never pulled out a body.

What?

I know what I saw. It was an arm! Somebody's arm!

They chatted with her for a while longer and then they headed towards their cars and drove away. She waved and smiled but once they disappeared, so did her grin.

She shut her trunk, folded her arms over her chest, and then looked in the direction of my house. Slowly I released the blinds, hoping that she hadn't seen me. I waited a while and by the next time I looked outside again, Blonde Jane was gone.

I called Brice, but he didn't answer, so I pulled his gun out of the night stand and headed downstairs to check to make sure that the new alarm system was turned on.

After I was comfortable on the couch, I replayed the vision of the arm coming out of the trunk, repeatedly, in my head.

"I know what I saw. I know what I saw."

Later that evening, I'd tried to bring Brice up to speed on everything, but he acted as though I was crazy. He'd said that if someone had been in Blonde Jane's trunk, then the police would have found them. But I know what I saw. But Brice wasn't convinced.

"Just move already Jane," Charity said in frustration, once I arrived at work the next day.

"It's not that simple."

"Yes it is. Find a house. Rent the house. And just let your house sit there until you are ready to sell it. I don't know what Brice makes, but I've seen your paychecks lady. So, I know that you can afford it," she laughed. "I'm sorry. It's not funny. Seriously, everyday it's something else. Something even more bizarre than the day before. Just convince him that it's best to leave. Personally, I would've been gone as soon as I found out that everyone had the same name. Jane, that's creepy," she shivered, and held up the newspaper. She read something aloud, but I was focused on the picture on the front of it.

"Let me see that," I asked and once she handed me the paper, I stared at the missing woman's photograph. It was the lady that had given me the realtor's card; at the coffee shop in Raleigh. The one in medical school. The one that I'd ran into at the gas station the other day.

They said that no one had seen or heard from her in a few days. A few days ago, I'd seen her at the gas station. A few days ago she'd told me that she'd been paid to give me the realtor's card. And then yesterday I saw an arm in the back of Blonde Jane's car.

No…that wasn't her arm…right?

I shook my head. But what if it was?

What if they'd been the one to give her the card?

To give to me? What if they'd been following me or something and saw me talking to her? What if they thought that she'd told me something that I wasn't supposed to know? Which in a way, I guess she had.

My stomach started to turn and I swallowed the lump of guilt in my throat. I'd made the woman talk to me. I hoped nothing had happened to her because of me.

"Jane? What's wrong?"

Glancing up from the paper, I saw the Red-haired Jane standing in front of our office window. She didn't move once I looked at her. She just stood there, with an evil smirk on her face.

"I think I'm going to be sick," I mumbled as I ran to towards the office bathroom.

Of course, they were probably following me. How else would they have known where I worked? From the looks of it, they were watching me just as much as I was watching them. Only, they weren't normal and them watching and following me was more than creepy.

My phone rang, and I answered it.

"Calling the police on me Jane wasn't a nice thing to do." It was her. Blonde Jane. "Didn't your mother ever teach you not to play with fire? Darling, you are bound to get burned," and with that she hung up. I was so frustrated, that I couldn't say or do anything. For a long while, I just stood there. Finally, I pulled myself together, and headed back out to my desk.

Charity stared at me with concern as I made myself comfortable. At the sound of the bell, I looked towards the door.

"Good morning Leo."

"Good morning ladies."

"What brings you by? We were just about to work on some ideas for your company."

"Well, that's what I'm here to talk about. It has come to our attention, that Mrs. Adams has some history that my company, nor I, want to be a part of or associated with," he said in a dry tone.

I was Mrs. Adams. Mary Jane Adams.

"Excuse me? And what kind of history are you referring to?"

"I'm not at liberty to say, but I don't want you or your name a part of the project. Ms. Dalton, if you would like to continue working with us, that's fine, we are going to need some new contracts. I'm sorry Mrs. Adams, but I have a reputation to keep," he stated bluntly.

I looked at him confused. My background was as clean as a whistle! I'd never been arrested. Hell, I'd never even had a speeding ticket, so what could he possibly be referring to?

"This has to be a mistake."

"I'm afraid it isn't."

"I'm sorry, but we are partners. Jane is really, really, good at what she does, and I don't think that I'll be able to complete the project without her," Charity spoke up.

"Okay, then. Suit yourself. We will find someone else. Good day ladies," and we watched over $50,000 of work, walk out of our office door.

"Ahhh!" I screamed, startling Charity and our few employees came running to the front of the office.

"She's fine. Get back to work."

"That bitch!"

"What bitch?"

"She did this!"

"Who did what?"

"Jane. The blonde one. She did this!" I was furious but I couldn't say that I was in disbelief.

"Wait, Jane. You really think so? Why would she do something like this? How could she do something like this?"

"How? I don't know how, but I know that she did it! She just called me and told me that I was playing with fire and that I would get burned. She knew that I'd called the police over to her house yesterday. And remember when I told you that she'd said that "The Janes" ran this city. Maybe she actually meant it. Maybe she knows Mr. Leo or something. Who knows. But we bought that house, I didn't sign up for this! And to tarnish my name and interfere with my business and my career. Oh, she was asking for trouble!" I roared, as I grabbed my purse and headed out of the office.

Brice was off that day, so I headed home. I drove towards the lane of terror and once I arrived, I sped into the driveway. Almost every Jane on our lane was standing on the sidewalk, in front of my house, watching Brice mow the lawn.

"Excuse me, but what the hell are you doing?" I asked them.

"We were taking a little stroll. Now, we're on break," the Latino Jane snickered.

I looked at Brice.

His shirt was off and he had on his head phones. He probably didn't even know that they were standing there.

"Get the hell away from my yard!"

"Last time I checked, the sidewalk isn't exactly included with your property. I should know. We should do lunch soon. Or dinner. We're all going to dinner Friday night, if you want to come," Blonde Jane suggested.

"That's never going to happen! So, STOP asking me! And I know that it was you. You said something to one of my clients, didn't you? I don't know what you could have possibly told him, but whatever it was, I'm sure that it wasn't the truth!"

"Excuse me?"

"You lied to him and as a result he pulled out of one of our projects! Admit it! Didn't you!" I screamed at her.

"Wouldn't you like to know," she answered sarcastically. "Now, come to dinner with us Jane."

I growled at her. "I don't know what kind of crazy shit that you, all of you, do around here, but when you mess with my clients, you're messing with my money! And I don't play about my money! I swear, I'm about two seconds from slapping that stupid ass grin off of your face! Keep messing with me Jane! Keep on and I promise you that I'm going to bless you with an ass whoopin'! Keep on!"

"Ohh, oh my, I'm so scared," she said with a smirk.

"If I were you, I would be! Hear me loud and hear me clear, these little games that you are playing, need to stop. Now!"

"Burn, Baby. Burn!" She giggled and I knew that she was being a smart ass.

"Oh, so you think this a joke?" I asked her, dropping my purse and my keys to the ground.

"As I told you before, we run this town sweetie. So, either get onboard or…"

"Or what?" I walked closer and closer to her. None of the other Janes said a word. They didn't move from her side, but they didn't say anything either.

"Or you'll be on my bad side. And you don't want to be on my bad side," she said.

"Oh, but I do. And I'll prove it!" Before she could reply, I pushed her.

"Jane!"

Brice screamed my name behind me and I already knew that he was headed in my direction.

"Why so angry? I know a really good counselor if you need to talk to someone. Anger doesn't look good on you. And this type of behavior isn't tolerated towards another Jane. Have you no understanding of sisterhood?" Blonde Jane resumed her posture and fixed her dress.

"I am not your damn sister!" I screamed at her.

"Come on baby. Let's go inside."

"Bye Jane. Dinner is Friday. 7 p.m. sharp. At the tavern on Peach Street. We would love it if you could make it. See you there. Don't be late," she blurted out behind me.

Once we were inside, Brice shut the door behind me.

"Jane. What the hell was that?"

"Do you know that a client backed out on us today? He stated that something came up about my past and he said that he didn't want his company associated with me."

"What? You've never so much as had a speeding ticket."

"That's what I said. So, I know that the Janes had something to do with it. She just basically admitted. I don't know what she said, but somehow, she got to him," I confirmed.

"Okay, babe, I think you're giving them way too much credit. They may be a little crazy and all but I doubt that they had anything to do with that."

"Don't doubt them. Don't doubt anything about them; especially the blonde one. And she laughed! Like it was one big joke or game to her!" I was burning with fury and I couldn't stop pacing back and forth.

"It sounded like they were trying to invite you to dinner to me."

"Are you taking their side?" I was already seeing red and Brice backed up just a little as he noticed my fists.

"No. Of course not. I just think you want them to be a bigger problem than what they are."

"Brice! Listen to me! She called me and told me that she knew that I was the one that sent the police to her house. Then she said that I was playing with fire and that I was going to get burned. And then all of a sudden, Mr. Leo shows up and pulls out of working with us. They are doing this Brice! You have to believe me!"

"I believe you. I just don't understand is all."

"She didn't deny it. And remember, the other day, the woman from the…"

Brice held up his finger.

"Babe, I'm sorry. Hold that thought. It's work. I need to take this," he said, and he answered the phone.

I rolled my eyes and glanced out of the window. All of the Janes were gone. They were probably somewhere plotting their next move against me.

"Now what were you saying?" Brice asked all of fifteen minutes later.

"We're moving," was all I said, and Brice didn't say anything for a while.

"Moving where?"

“You don’t worry about anything. You worry about work, and I’ll worry about finding us a place to stay. I still don’t feel my best. I’m going to bed,” I mumbled as I walked up the stairs with him following behind me.

“I’ll come put you to sleep,” he flirted.

“No thanks,” I turned him down and shut the bathroom door behind me. I heard him groan but he didn’t say another word. And for the rest of the day, neither did I.

After taking medicine, late that night, around 2 a.m. I woke up to use the bathroom. I noticed that Brice wasn’t in bed, so I headed downstairs to find him. He’d fallen asleep on the couch, with his laptop on his chest.

I thought about waking him up with a little mouth-action, but his snores confirmed that what he needed the most at that moment was rest. I turned off the lamp. And headed to lie on the other couch, but suddenly, I heard chatter.

The Janes.

They were all holding a lit candle and chatting with each other as they walked. I looked at the time again. It was now 2:07 a.m. but all of them were still fully dressed and slowly walking towards Blonde Jane’s back yard. I held my breath, watching them, until the very last Jane was out of sight.

"Just go to bed Jane. Just go to bed."

I didn't think going over was the best idea, since I feared that I might not come back, but I did decide to step out on the front porch, just to see if I heard chanting or praying, or something that might explain their craziness…but I didn't.

All I heard was…laughter.

Huh?

~*************************~

CHAPTER FOUR

"Brice, your phone is ringing. Who's calling you so late?" Brice groaned and I reached to pick up his phone.

"Hello," I mumbled.

"Yes. We're looking for Brice Adams. There has been a fire at his business. Artz Inc. We need him to get here right away," I heard him say as the phone dropped from my hands and I screamed at Brice. Within five minutes we were pulling out of our driveway, and he turned an hour drive into less than thirty minutes.

"What happened?" Brice asked as soon as his feet hit the pavement. It was gone. There was nothing there but smoke and ashes. The entire building had been burn to the ground.

"The flames were out of control by the time we got here. There was nothing that we could do," the firefighter confessed as Brice dropped his head.

We spent hours at the scene, though there was nothing worth savaging. I seemed to be more upset than Brice was. Things like this just didn't happen to us. We were good people. Always had been. We had a good life. A perfect life. Before we bought that house.

"I'm sorry Brice," I said, breaking the silence between us as we drove back towards home.

"It's okay. There was nothing no one could have done. Insurance will cover everything. I'll just get a new building and start over. Thank goodness I have everything backed up to my home computer."

"Do you really believe that it was an electrical problem?"

"You heard what they said Jane. The building was old. I'm sure it was just an electrical problem."

"Maybe. Or maybe it was a "Jane" problem," I said.

"Look, not this again, okay. Those women are weird, I'll give you that, but to think that they caused this fire, to my business, is just absurd! You're becoming obsessed with this whole "The Janes" thing and I don't like it. I don't like it at all!" Brice chastised me.

"But…"

"But nothing Jane! I don't want to hear it! You don't want to stay in the house, fine. I get it. We will find a house by the end of the week," he said before turning up the radio and acting as though I wasn't even there for the rest of the drive.

We arrived home just as the sun started to rise. Brice rushed inside and I just sat in the car, wondering if he was right. What if I was making things more than they were? Nope. I was right. Because only five short minutes later, I saw her, Blonde Jane, pull into her driveway. She rushed out of her car and into her house.

So, she just happened to be up at the break of dawn, on the same morning that my husband's business was burnt to the ground?

I think not!

I opened the car door and just as I took two steps towards the road, Brice called my name.

"Jane." He said standing in the doorway and waited for me to turn around and come inside.

I didn't care if no one believed me, I was right about Blonde Jane and the rest of the crew; and I was going to prove it.

~***~

I arrived home just in time to see Silent Jane coming from my backyard.

"What the hell are you doing?"

She smiled. "Hey Jane."

"Don't hey me. What the hell were you doing in my backyard?"

She was quiet.

"Answer me damn it!" I screamed at her but she still didn't speak. Instead, she pointed behind her.

A small dog came waddling in our direction.

"When did you get a dog?"

She didn't answer me. She spoke to the dog instead. "Come on Jane. Come to Mommy."

Oh no! Not the damn dog too! This Jane Name thing was just way too serious!

"She ran into your backyard. I went to get her. Have a good day Jane," she finally said to me and then she scurried on her way. I checked the backyard just to make sure everything was in place. It was. I could only assume that she hadn't tried to get inside of the house because the alarm would've sounded and the security company would've notified us. But I made a mental note to watch the video footage once I was inside.

I headed back around to the front yard to find Blond Jane waiting for me.

"Ugh, what do you want?" I rolled my eyes.

"A little birdie told me that you are trying to rent a house on Mulberry Street. We really like you around here Jane and we want you to stay," she said as though she was sincere.

"Just stop the bs, okay? You don't like me, and I damn sure don't like you."

"Why?"

"Something is wrong with you. All of you. But especially you. My guess is that you're a psychopath or something. I can't prove it. But I know that I'm right about you. I know that all of the crazy and weird things that have been happening around here and to me, and my husband. I know that it's all because of you. And I know that you had a body in your trunk. I don't care if no one believes me, you and I both know the truth and I know that you are up to no good."

"I only have your best interest at heart Jane. I can assure you of that. I want us to be friends," she smiled.

Her smile made me nauseous. It was evil, sarcastic, and personally, I just wanted to punch her and be done with it already.

"Could you get the hell out of my yard please? I have some packing to do." I'd been looking at rentals like crazy and packing up the house at the same time. At this point, I didn't care where we went, as long as we off of S.J. Lane, I would be just fine. Even if I didn't absolutely love the house that I was about to go see, I was taking it.

"Packing? But you're not going anywhere Jane. I can promise you that you'll be staying right here Jane, with us."

"We'll see about that." I turned my back to her.

"Oh my, you've picked up a little weight. You aren't pregnant, are you?"

"And if I am? That's none of your damn business," I said to her, suddenly feeling uncomfortable.

"Oh, but I would hate for it to become my business."

"Excuse me?" I turned back around to face her. "If my husband and I are expecting a baby, that's none of your concern! There are plenty of couples on this street with kids and…"

"Have you ever seen them?"

"No. I haven't. But I've heard them."

"You heard what we wanted you to hear."

What?

I looked around S.J. Lane.

"What are you saying? That there are no children on S.J. Lane? What about the toys and bicycles in the yards?"

"You saw what you wanted to see."

"But at the barbeque, you said that they weren't invited."

"They aren't. Not to our barbeques. And not on S.J. Lane. We like to keep a certain look on our street. Children make women weak. And we don't have any room for weakness. We took a vote. You should know better than to believe everything that you see Jane. But, image is everything. The *perfect* image is everything. Maybe you should try the pill. I'll text you the name of a really good one. Hopefully it isn't too late," Blonde Jane offered.

"No. Don't text me a damn thing!" I bellowed and I turned to walk away from her but glanced at her over my shoulder to tell her one last thing. "By the way, has anyone ever told you that your breath smells like dog shit?" And with that I hurried up the steps and into the house. I relaxed up against the door as I thought about the things that she'd said.

So, they pretended to have kids?

To keep up some perfect image?

That explains why I never saw them. I recalled images of the yards with the toys thrown all over them. It was all for show. It was all smoke and mirrors.

Why? I wasn't sure. And at this point, I didn't care!

I killed a little time by packing up a few more things before it was time to head to meet the owner of the rental.

I drove fast, lost in my thoughts and it wasn't until the blue lights flashed in my rearview mirror, that I realized that I was going over 80 mph. Well, there goes my perfect driving record.

I pulled over and the cop car pulled over behind me. I pulled out my license and retrieved my registration, and waited for him to approach my car. I glanced back at him, assuming that he was running my license plate, but after another minute or so, suddenly he turned off his blue lights, and a few seconds later, he simply pulled off and drove away.

What?

For a few minutes, I sat there, unsure of what to do, but when he didn't return, I headed towards the rental on Mulberry Street. I arrived at the rental property fifteen minutes early and once the owner was thirty minutes late, I called him. But he didn't answer. I texted him and waited for his reply, but he never responded and he never showed up.

I guess Blonde Jane had found a way to get to him, but I didn't get discouraged. She may have won this battle, but I'd be damned if I let her win the war!

~***~

"No, Brice, not right now."

"Why? Because you're so busy staring out of the window?" I could hear the frustration in his voice.

But I didn't want to have sex. I was watching the Janes.

Unfortunately, we were still in the house. Every rental property that I'd even tried to go and see, was somehow sabotaged. Either the owners never showed up or they always ended up calling to cancel.

"It's been over a week Jane," Brice reminded me that we hadn't been intimate as he kissed the back of my neck. But I kept my eyes outside. The Janes were skipping back and forth from each other's houses and I was sure that if I even blinked, I'd probably miss something.

"Did you hear what I just said?"

"Yes. And I'll be sure to have sex with you later tonight. Okay?"

Brice exhaled, but he didn't respond. I heard him grab his keys, walk down the stairs, and then soon after that, the front door slammed shut.

I stayed in the single chair by our bedroom window. I exhaled as I watched him drive away. I stayed by the window, and after a while, I saw Blonde Jane go into her house, and come out with a pie. She headed towards my house. I watched her and listened for a knock on the door, but the knock never came. Instead, I saw Blonde Jane head back across the street, empty-handed.

What is she up to?

I headed downstairs and opened the front door.

The pie was sitting on the porch right in front of it. I picked it up and studied it. It didn't smell as good as the other one had. Actually, it didn't smell like cherries at all. I touched the dark red drippings and it wasn't long before I figure out that the filling…was blood.

I dropped the pie and all at once, laughter exploded from every direction. All of the Janes, each and every one of them, were standing on their front porches, looking in my direction, laughing hysterically. Even Silent Jane was cackling from next door.

"You sick and twisted Bitches!" I stormed into the house and locked the door behind me. I called Brice over and over again until finally, he answered. I told him that I needed him to come back home immediately. I scrubbed my hands and I waited impatiently for Brice to arrive.

"What? What's wrong?"

"You didn't see that?"

"See what?"

"On the porch? It's blood."

"Where?"

I smacked my lips as he followed me back out of the door. But abruptly, I stopped. The blood-filled pie…was gone.

~***~

Day after day, it was as though the Janes were intentionally trying to drive me crazy. It was always something. Knocks on the front door, and when I would answer it, no one would be there. My car alarm going off repeatedly throughout the night. Dead animals randomly showing up in our yard. Clients at work backing out of projects, left and right. And the list goes on.

I complained and whined to Brice every single day, but he never seemed as bothered. I guess it was because nothing was happening to him---except the fire, which he still believed was an accident. But the truth was that the Janes had caused it. They were causing everything.

On the bright side, I was thankful that I wasn't pregnant. Though I'd always wanted a baby, now just wasn't the time. I assumed that my period was just late due to stress and maybe that was even to blame for my sudden weight gain. Nevertheless, that negative pregnancy test was the best thing that had happened to me in a very long time.

"Who is that?" Brice asked as my phone ranged over and over again.

"Probably the Janes; one of them. They do that. Call me over and over again, all day, from different numbers."

Brice exhaled. Whenever I so much as mentioned the Janes, he immediately got an attitude.

"Fine, if you don't believe me, next time answer it."

Seconds later, the phone ranged again. Brice picked it up. I listened to his responses, and then he reached me the phone.

"Hello?"

They giggled, and then hung up the phone.

"Told you."

"Told me what? That was a potential client. She said that she'd come across your ad on the internet."

I shook my head. "That wasn't a client Brice. That was the Janes."

Brice sat on the bed to put on his shoes. "I think you should drive down to your parents this weekend. Just to clear your head," Brice suggested.

Lately, on most days, he and I weren't seeing eye to eye, but that was only because he didn't believe me. And that was a problem, which in turn, caused us other problems.

"Oh. So, you're trying to get rid of me?"

"No. But the way that you have been acting lately, I…"

"You what? You don't want me here Brice?"

"I didn't say that Jane."

"But you wanted to."

He grunted. "Did I say that Jane? Did I? Damn!"

"See. This is what I'm talking about. We're arguing and fighting over stupid shit! This isn't us Brice."

"You're right. It isn't. I have enough stress on my plate as it is and…I just want my wife back. Not this crazy, obsessed person that you've become," Brice said and with that, he grabbed his keys and was gone.

I didn't chase after him, or even call him. He wasn't the only one dealing with stress. And I was tired of him making me out to be the problem. The Janes were the problem. Not me.

I spent the rest of the day, alone and reflecting. I didn't go to work. I didn't do anything. I didn't even remember falling asleep that night, but when I woke up the next morning, Brice still wasn't there.

It was Friday, and I returned Charity's calls, only to tell her that I wouldn't be coming in again. I hadn't been to the office at all, the whole week, but still, as always, Charity said that it was okay, but I knew that it wasn't. I knew that I had to pull myself together, or I would end up losing my business partner, and probably my husband too.

I skimmed through the 174 missed calls on my phone and out of all of them, only 1 of them was from Brice. The rest were from the many unsaved numbers that belonged to the women of S.J. Lane.

After listening to Brice's voicemail, telling me that he was staying at a friend's the night before, I got myself together and checked outside before heading out. I didn't want to run into any of them. I literally ran to my car and hurried out of the driveway. I had no idea where I was going but I knew that I wasn't going to my parent's house. I didn't want them to know that Brice and I were having problems.

I'd been gone all of five minutes, and my phone started to ring.

"Oh, my God!" I frowned. I thought about having my number changed, again, but that only usually worked for about a day. Somehow, the very next day, they would have my new number, and they never hesitated to use dial it.

I just didn't understand.

What is it that they wanted from me?

On the fifth call, with an attitude, finally, I answered my phone.

"Are you ready to play nice, Jane?"

I wasn't sure which Jane it was, but it wasn't the Blonde one and I didn't answer her question. I just hung up.

Play nice? Nope. It was time for me to play dirty.

It was time for me to find out some truth.

I found a local coffee shop, ordered and found a table.

"Let's see what I can find," I said, typing "The Janes" in the search tab on my phone. A musical group came up, but that's not what I needed so I searched "Janes in Smithfield, North Carolina." Still nothing specific that I could use. I searched for the Blonde Jane by her legal name, Jane Peterson, and narrowing down the search by her address, I found out that her maiden name was Jane Lee Kincaid.

Wait a minute, what is that?

I found that she was also listed as Jane Kincaid Jordan, until a few years ago. So, she was married before. And we still had a Jane Jordan on S.J. Lane…were they past in-laws? Maybe the sister of the previous husband?

I studied the *Whitepage listing* with the names and past information for a while and then I took a screenshot of it.

"Is anyone sitting here?"

I looked up from my phone. A tall, stallion of a man, towered over me. He awaited my response, but all I could do was shake my head no.

He took a seat and sipped his coffee in silence.

Finally forcing myself to stop staring at him, I turned my attention back towards my phone, but suddenly I got an idea.

"Are you from Smithfield?"

He nodded. "Born and raised."

So, then he must have heard of the Janes, right?

"Have you ever heard of the Janes?"

"Of course. I've heard plenty of stories about them. Why do you ask?"

"Um, I'm a reporter. And I wanted to do a story on the number of women named Jane in this town. My friend brought it to my attention, and I thought it would be an interesting piece."

"Well, good luck. There are so many women named Jane around here. Did you pay attention to the cashier's name tag? Even her name is Jane."

I glanced at the cashier. I hadn't even paid her name tag any attention.

"You didn't even notice it, did you? And you call yourself a reporter?" He laughed and so did I. "From what I know about them, decades ago, there was a fad. All of the wealthy women were naming their first-born daughters, Jane. They say that some even gave the name "Jane" to all of their daughters, just for the hell of it. The Janes have been around for years and being that most of them come from wealth, they are tied to a lot of women and men in high positions and with important roles; politicians, doctors, judges, lawyers, law enforcement---you name it. But all Janes aren't the same. There are the Janes that are wealthy or from wealth, and hold some kind of value or importance around here; and then there are those that are just *regular* Janes, whose parents decided to join in on the fad," he commented nodded at the cashier.

"Have they been known to be dangerous?"

"You never hear of them being in any trouble. Most folks say to stay out of their way, and you'll never know that they exist. They pretty much stay to themselves and don't blend much with normal folks, yet everyone knows who they are. They do news articles on them from time to time, highlighting them for their charity work or contributions. It's a lot of them though.

"Really?"

"Yep. They live in different communities, all over the city," he concluded as he took another sip of his coffee. And for the next ten minutes or so, we continued to chat.

He talked about the town and things of that nature. He even managed to make me laugh a few times, which I hadn't done in a while.

Finally, we both stood to leave and he opened the door for me to walk outside.

"I never got your name, Ms. Reporter."

He smiled and I laughed.

"Well…it's Jane."

"What? No kidding!" He laughed as I nodded and then he extended a hand.

"Well, nice to meet you, Ms. Jane," he said and as I shook his hand he kissed mine. Immediately, I stiffened.

"Maybe we could do coffee again sometime," he suggested.

"Sorry, I don't think so. Actually, it's Mrs. Jane. I'm married." I was sure that he'd noticed the ring on my finger. But maybe again, he hadn't.

"Happily?"

"Absolutely," I answered hastily.

He stared at me. And then he pulled out a card.

"Good. Well, if you ever change your mind, about that cup of *Joe*," he handed me the card and walked away. As soon as I was to my car, I threw the card down to the ground, before getting inside.

Just as I pulled off, I called my husband.

"So, you think that it's okay not to come home?"

"It was late. I slept at Andrew's. I'm sure you listened to my voicemail. Are you at your parents?"

"No."

"Are you at work?"

"No."

"Do you have plans to go to Charlotte for the weekend?"

"No."

"Well, I guess I should go ahead and tell you that I won't be coming home, tonight, again. Or for the whole weekend."

"What? Why?"

"We are so behind. I've been off my game for the past few days, so things on my end are slacking. Not to mention that there's still so much work to catch up on since the fire. We have deadlines that we are missing from left to right, and missed deadlines, means refunded money. Of course, they know what happened, but we still have obligations, and we still promised our services. Since Andrew has the home office and space, we're all going to be working here for the weekend; all day and all night. I'll be staying at the hotel down the street."

"What room? I'll just come there."

"No."

"No what Brice?"

"No, Jane. I don't want to argue with you this weekend. I have work to do. I'll barely be there anyway. It's just best if you don't come. Just don't come. I'll call you when I get the room," Brice said.

My feelings were hurt and without him knowing, I started to cry.

"Are you serious Brice? You don't want me to come? Really, are you serious?"

"Very."

"So, you just want me to stay at home, all alone, with those crazy people all around me?"

"Jane, you're more worried about them than they are about you. More than you are worried about us. Look, I gotta' go. I love you. I'll call you later," he said and waited on my reply but when I didn't say anything, he grunted and then hung up.

I threw my phone into the passenger seat. I didn't know how to feel. I thought briefly at the possibility that he could be having an affair, but I shook my head.

That wasn't his style. He was just angry at me. And probably horny too. But he was acting like I'd done something wrong and I didn't like it. I didn't like it at all!

As the rain started to fall, I headed towards home. I called Charity and asked her if she wanted to come over for the weekend, and I suggested that we too could use the time to catch up on all of the work that I'd missed. She told me that she could hear it in my voice that I needed her, so she agreed, and stated that once she left the office, and got her son settled at her sister's house, she would be on her way.

I spent most of my day crying, and texting Brice back to back messages of my feelings. We were so much happier before coming here. Things between us were so much better. And I didn't want to lose him. He was the best part of me, and no matter what, I couldn't lose him.

In a house that was silent and that had started to grow dark, I glanced at the clock. It was getting later into the evening, and Charity still hadn't shown up, and she wasn't answering her phone. I'd made up in my mind that if she didn't show up, I didn't care what Brice said, I was going to the hotel because I wasn't staying at home alone---again.

From the window, I stared at Silent Jane.

Here lately, I noticed that she'd been leaving her house, a lot more than usual. For a long while, she would barely even come outside, and now she was hardly ever home. Maybe she'd met someone. Though I'd never seen any man, or anyone at all for that matter at her house, she had to be going somewhere.

I watched her place the overnight bag into her car and then she drove away in a hurry. I wondered why she hadn't taken her dog with her. Maybe it wasn't an overnight bag---maybe it was a bag filled with something else.

It was a little after seven in the evening and after sitting in the same spot, a little while longer, I got a crazy idea. Silent Jane hadn't returned, and I wondered if she was gone for the night. I wondered if she had a spare key somewhere around her house. Most people did. And if we weren't in this neighborhood, with these people, I was sure that we would too. But if I could just get into her house, and take a look around, who knows what I would find.

Maybe something that I could use to prove to my husband that the Janes weren't who they were pretending to be.

I headed out of the back door. All was quiet, so I tip-toed towards Silent Jane's back porch.

I twisted the knob on her back door. Of course, it was locked, so I looked around, wondering where she might hide a key.

I could hear her dog barking as I searched. It was small, so I figured that it wouldn't cause any problems.

I moved a few things around as the dog continued to bark and then suddenly, I heard a voice.

"Jane, what are you barking at?" she asked.

What?

I damn near broke my neck trying to run back to my house as fast as I could. After I made it inside, I locked the back door, and rushed to the living room out of breath.

That was Silent Jane's voice but I hadn't heard her car pull into the driveway and looking outside, it wasn't there.

Huh?

I headed to the kitchen to get a different view of her house. Still no car, and all of the lights in her house were off.

Confused, I grabbed my keys and slowly walked to my car as if I had somewhere to go. I didn't, but I wanted to look at Silent Jane's house from the front.

I'd seen her put a bag into her car. I'd seen her drive away. Her car still wasn't there. All of her lights were off.

But she was there. I'd heard her voice. I'd heard her loud and clear.

But where was her car? Had she parked somewhere and walked back home? But why? Why was she pretending as though she wasn't there? Why was she sitting in the dark?

An eerie feeling hit me all at once, but somewhat I felt relieved as Charity's truck pulled in behind me. As Charity made her way to my car, still, I sat there, staring at Silent Jane's house. I knew that she was watching. From a window, in the dark, I knew that she was there.

"Do you ever want to get married again?" I asked Charity. Friday night we'd caught up on work, and now Saturday night was all about girl talk, getting drunk and relaxing.

"Maybe. If I met the right guy. These days, there aren't too many options," she sipped her wine.

"Do you miss sex?"

"Who said that I wasn't having sex? Why do you think I was late getting here yesterday?" She laughed.

"Humph, and I guess you conveniently forgot to tell your best friend about this new sex partner huh," I laughed.

"But seriously, I don't know what I would do if Brice and I got a divorce. He's all that I know. I hate how things are between us."

"They'll get better. Once you are out of this house, and out of this neighborhood, things will go back to normal."

"I hope so. We can't even find anyone who will rent to us. And not just in Smithfield. Every house that we've tried even look at, whether in this town or back in Raleigh, the owners never showed up. And I know that it's not just by coincidence. It's them," I said, knowing that Charity knew who I was referring to. "I'd done a little digging on them, but I hadn't found much. The only thing I found out was that Blonde Jane has an ex-husband.

"He probably left her because her ass is crazy."

"Probably. Or because her breath smells like burnt dick."

"Wait a minute. Now, what in the hell does burnt dick smell like?" Charity squealed.

"Girl, I don't know. I just know that it has got to be one hell of a bad smell," I chucked. Suddenly, there was a knock at the door. We headed towards the door it together.

"I was coming by to invite you over for drinks, but I see that the party has already started," the Latino Jane said.

"No! No! No! I don't know how many times I have to say it. NO! I don't want to talk to, drink with, go with, laugh with, do anything with, any of you. Could you please pass the message? Please!" Clearly, I was drunk; but I'd meant every word that I'd said. I felt Charity elbow me.

"Sure. We will come," she said to Latino Jane and I looked back at her confused.

"Sorry. Only Jane is invited," she said.

"And why is that?" Charity asked.

"Because she's a Jane."

Charity stepped in front of me. "So. What's so special about being a Jane?" Charity was drunk too, but I was glad that she was asking questions that I also wanted to know the answers to.

"What isn't?" Latino Jane stood her ground.

Charity rambled for a while and then she poked Latino Jane's arm.

"Eww! Eww! Eww! Eww! Eww! You touched me!" Latino Jane became hysterical as she rubbed the spot on her arm where Charity touched her. "Eww! Oh, my God! Eww! Eww! Eww!" She continued to rub her arm as though Charity's touch was infectious. She took off running and skipping, still screaming in disgust and rubbing the "infected" spot along the way.

"Girl…what the hell just happened?" Charity asked me. But all I could do was shake my head and shrug.

~***~

Brice sat on the couch beside of me to eat his food. He didn't make jokes or even bother to say anything at all. He just ate his dinner as though I wasn't even there.

"Brice?"

"Andrew knows someone who has a house coming open soon. It's in Raleigh. I don't know if you want to move back that far from your job, but once it's open, I'm taking it. I've already talked to the owner. We've already worked out the pricing. As soon as it's ready, we can move in."

"Do you want me to come with you?" I asked him as though my heart had been broken.

"You're my wife Jane. Why wouldn't I?"

I was quiet. I knew that taking a house back in Raleigh meant that I would be back to a longer commute, but at this point, I didn't care. I was just happy that he was trying to find a way out of this.

"What about the house?"

"I'm not worried about this house. I'm worried about us and what being here is doing to you. What it's doing to us. Screw this house Jane. We'll sell it when we can. Even if we lose out on money."

I smiled at him and just as he took another bite of his food, I kissed him.

"I'm sorry…" Before I could finish my sentence, the doorbell sounded.

"I'll get it," Brice said.

I watched him as he opened the door, but no one was there. He bent over and when he stood back up, he was holding an envelope.

"What's that?"

He shrugged as he opened it.

I looked on as he pulled out the contents and flipped through them.

"Jane what is this?"

Brice walked towards me.

I waited on him to say something else.

"You went on a date? With another man?"

What?

"What is that? Let me see."

"Answer my question. Are you cheating on me Jane?"

"What? No."

I waited on him to hand me the papers, but he held them tightly as I tried to pull them from him.

"Brice. I'm not cheating on you. I would never cheat on you."

"Then explain this!" Brice screamed and threw the papers in my face. I hurriedly collected them.

They were pictures of me. Sitting in the coffee shop with the gentleman that asked to sit at the table. There were pictures of us talking and laughing and of him walking me outside. There was also a picture of him kissing my hand.

"It's not what you think."

"Who is he Jane? Who the fuck is he?"

"I don't know. I'd never seen him before that day."

"Stop lying Jane! Do I look stupid to you? You never met him but you're smiling in every damn picture and he's kissing your hand! But he was just some random man, right? Some stranger? Who the hell is he Jane!"

I jumped as he yelled my name. I tried to answer him but every time I opened my mouth to speak, he cut me off and screamed something else.

"Brice! It's not what you think!"

I looked down at the photos of me again.

Who in the hell took these pictures?

The pictures were from a distance.

Whoever took them had to have been watching me. Whoever took them…was a Jane!

That's it! This was the last straw!

Screwing with me was one thing, but trying to screw with my marriage was another!

With Brice still yelling, barefoot and all, I stormed past him and headed outside. Blonde Jane was standing at the end of her driveway, obviously listening to Brice and I arguing. She was probably the one who'd left the pictures at the door and if she wasn't, she knew who had. She saw me coming towards her, and she even had the audacity to smile.

"Hello Jane," she said.

"You bitch!"

"Well that's not a very nice thing to say," she smiled.

"How dare you follow me and take pictures to give to my husband!"

"What pictures Jane? I don't know what you're talking about," she replied innocently but I didn't respond. Instead, I lunged at her. I grabbed her by the throat and I squeezed. She pushed and pulled, but I squeezed harder.

"Why won't you just leave me the hell alone!"

As I screamed at her, she tried to peel my fingers from around her throat but when she couldn't get me to loosen my grip, she punched me so hard that I stopped breathing for a little over a second. And then, all hell broke loose.

Everything from there was pretty much a blur.

Blonde Jane and I went blow for blow and it wasn't until Brice was pulling me by the waist, that I came to and realized that Blonde Jane and I were both bleeding.

"Stay the hell out of my business!" I yelled at her as I lunged forward again but Brice picked me up off of my feet. I noticed her husband standing on the front porch, but he hadn't come down to assist her. He sipped his drink as though he was happy that someone had finally stood up to her.

"You have no idea who you're dealing with," she growled but I told her to kiss my ass as Brice carried me across the street.

Once we were in our yard, Brice put me down.

"Get the fuck in the house Jane! Now! I said get in the house!"

I walked towards the door and I saw Brice walk towards his car. I stood on the porch and watched Brice drive away. I wanted to drive behind him, but I knew that it was no use. He wouldn't listen to a thing that I had to say. He probably wouldn't even talk to me. But he would read his text messages.

Going in to find my phone, I slammed the front door so hard that a picture fell from the wall. I found my phone and then sat on the couch and waited. I figured that Blonde Jane would probably call the police or something but surprisingly, she didn't. The police never came.

The sun went down and I was still sitting in the same spot, all alone. I'd texted Brice a thousand times, but he hadn't responded. Not even once.

All was quiet outside. No one had even come out of their houses for hours.

I headed to the kitchen and grabbed a bottle of vodka. The first gulp felt like Christmas morning and an hour later, with the bottle still in my hand, I grabbed my car keys and wobbled outside to my car.

"Screw this! I'm going to find my husband. Brice, I'm coming to find you," I sang, drunker than I'd been only a few nights before. I managed to make it to my car. But that was about it. I couldn't even figure out how to start it, so, I just sat there, with the doors locked, drinking and crying as I sang pieces of our "first dance" song from our wedding. And after a while, everything went dark.

The next morning, I woke up to the sun beaming in on my face. After throwing up, I noticed Brice sitting on the front porch. It was still early morning. No one else appeared to be up or out.

“I shook you, but you were passed out,” Brice mumbled.

“How long have you been sitting here?”

“Hours. How did you end up in the car?”

“I was going to find you. But I was too drunk.”

“Why would you be trying to drive drunk Jane? You know better than that. Anything could’ve happened.”

“So. It’s not like you would’ve cared anyway.” I whined.

Brice exhaled.

“You don’t really believe that, do you? I don’t know what I would do if I lost you,” he confirmed.

My heart started to melt as I inched toward him.

“I saw your text messages. We used to tell each other everything. It just looked like…”

“I know how it looked, but I swear, he asked for a seat. I asked him about the Janes. He made a few jokes and then he walked me outside.”

“And kissed your hand.” Brice looked at me angrily. I mean, he was acting as though the man had given my hand a blow job or something.

“Yes. I shook his hand and he kissed mine. But it was all innocent,” I explained to him. I didn’t bother to tell him about the coffee invite. It was no point in stirring the pot. “I know you don't want to hear this, but seeing the pictures, maybe the Janes sent him in my direction. I don't know. And whether you believe me or not, I know that they had something to do with it."

Brice didn't respond. Instead, he stood up.

"Let's just go, please! Today! I don't care about the house. I don't care about how much money we lose. I just care about you. Please. We can go to a hotel until whenever. Please, let's just go," I begged him.

Brice walked closer to me and wiped my tears.

"Okay."

"Really?"

"Yes."

I couldn't begin to express how happy I was, but hurriedly, we headed inside to get a few things to take with us to the hotel. We'd agreed that we would stay in the hotel until the rental, through Brice's friend Andrew, was ready. We packed in silence. I knew that things weren't going to go back to normal overnight, but getting out of this house was a start.

Brice continued to get things together and I headed downstairs to find my phone. I searched the living room and then I remembered that the last time I'd seen it was when I'd text Brice the night before, right after opening the bottle of vodka. So, I headed to the kitchen.

"Shit!" I jumped at the sight of her.

Red-haired Jane was sitting at the kitchen table.

"How the hell did you get into my house?"

She smiled. "I used my key."

"Key? What damn key? We changed the locks."

"All of our locks are the same Jane."

What?

"All of our houses use the same key."

"Bullshit! I had the locks changed!"

"No. He just pretended to change them and just made the both of you a new set…of your old keys. The locks are still the same. The locksmith is my uncle. I should know," She grinned as I forced myself to close my mouth.

What kind of shit is this!

"I came by to make peace. Yesterday got out of hand, but Jane forgives you. Janes don't fight each other. We stick together."

"Get out of my house."

"You're packing. Going somewhere?"

"What? How did you know that?"

"We know everything."

"Well, know this. No matter what you say, we're leaving and selling this house. Now…get…out!"

"Catch." Red-haired Jane said out of nowhere and she tossed something at me. Before I'd had time to even see what it was, I clasped the object in my hands.

My left hand started to sting and I noticed that it was a knife and that it had made a small cut in my palm.

Immediately, I dropped it.

"What the hell!" I yelled at her and placed my hand in the bottom of my shirt.

She moved quickly, and picked the knife up in a hurry.

"Who throws a knife at someone!"

"Not just a knife. A murder weapon. With your prints all over it," she said, wiggling her fingers at me. I hadn't noticed that she was wearing black gloves the whole time.

"What! What do you mean a murder weapon? For who?"

"That's for me to know. And for you to never find out, unless you don't follow the rules," she said. "We've been nice enough. Now, it's time for you to get in line Jane. Or suffer the consequences. Don't leave this house Jane. You belong here. With us. Forever!" And then she literally went running out of the back door.

I screamed for Brice and raced to the sink to wash my hand. I heard him running down the stairs.

"You didn't hear me yelling?"

"No. I was in the bathroom. What's wrong?"

After filling him in on what had just happened, Brice looked at my hand, and then he suggested that we called the police. But I told him that it was no use. I had a feeling that they had eyes and ears everywhere; including in the police station and in our house.

"She knew that we were packing. They are always two steps ahead of us. Somehow, they have to be listening." I started to look around the living room. I moved things around, and checked behind objects as Brice looked on. I couldn't tell if he really believed everything that I'd just told him, but he started to help me look anyway. "Check the smoke detectors."

Brice did as he was told.

"Babe," he said and pulled out a small mic.

"I told you! They've been listening to our conversations. This whole time!" I yelled as he ripped it from the smoke detector and headed to check the rest of them. I smirked once I heard him cursing and yelling and I just stood there with the "I told you these bitches were crazy" face, until he came back into the living room with a hand full of microphones.

He opened the door and tossed them outside.

"Now do you believe me?"

"Why? Why would they want to listen to our conversations?"

I shrugged. I walked towards the window to see if any of the Janes were headed towards our house, but all was clear.

I couldn't say that I was surprised but still, I was pissed! But the microphones and the matching door locks were the least of my worries.

"What about the knife Brice? It has my prints on it. What if she was serious about trying to use it against me?"

"Look, don't worry about that. I mean do you know how crazy and farfetched that sounds? She'll never be able to get away with something like that."

"Are you sure about that?" I said sarcastically.

"There's only one way to find out," Brice said, and he got on his phone to make a few calls. I watched him carry bag after bag to his car and not too long after that, we arrived at the hotel.

Brice had called our lawyer, to put him in the loop, and he said that we would just deal with everything else once it came our way.

I had been right. All along, I had been right.

They were sneaky, liars, and everything else in between. And I knew that they were capable of anything. And something told me that things were only going to get worse.

"Sir, I'm sorry, but your card declined," she said.

"That's impossible. Try this one."

She swiped and then shook her head. None of his cards were working, so I reached her mine.

"Sorry ma'am, yours didn't work either."

We looked at each other.

Okay Janes…

Let the games begin!

~**********************~

CHAPTER FIVE

"The bank has our accounts all figured out. They had no idea how the temporary hold had gotten on them in the first place," Brice said. "I'll be sure to pay Andrew back today."

"Okay. And please tell him that I said thank you too."

"Will do."

Brice stared at me.

"What's wrong?"

"I just can't seem to relax. I know that something is going to happen. I'm just waiting to see what it is. I know that they're going to pull something. For some reason, they want us at that house."

We'd been at the hotel for two days and I was still on edge. Remembering the Red-Haired Jane's last words, it seemed as though the Janes were determined to keep us on S.J. Lane.

Why they wanted us there so badly?

I wasn't sure yet. But I sure that they were probably trying to find a way to make us come back.

"I'm sorry that I didn't believe you from the start about them. I don't know why…I'm sorry baby."

"It's okay. I wish that you didn't have to go to work."

"I need to. I'll only be there for a few hours. You should be safe here. There's plenty of people around. The room is in Andrew's name, so you will be fine. Hang out at the bar or in the lobby if it will make you feel safer. Or, you could always ride with me. I won't be long."

I shook my head and he kissed my lips.

"I love you."

"You better."

And then he was gone.

I thought about calling Charity, since I hadn't called her, answered her calls, or been by the office, but I figured that I would wait until later. Instead, I decided to try and rest. I was still barely sleeping, but I forced myself to relax and at some point, or another, finally, I dozed off.

But not for long.

My heart skipped a beat at the sound of her voice.

"Housekeeping."

I opened my eyes in terror and there stood Blonde Jane and her sidekick; the Red-Haired one.

"Hello Jane."

I jumped to my feet so fast that it made me dizzy.

"What the hell are you doing here? And how did you get into my room?"

I looked for my phone to call for help, but it was gone. I opened the drawer beside the hotel bed. Brice's gun was gone too.

"We've come to take you home."

The hotel telephone was missing and I was starting to panic, but I didn't show it.

"Get the hell out of here! I'm not going anywhere with you!"

"Our society, is perfect. The Janes are perfect. We have perfect houses. Perfect husbands. Perfect communities. And that won't change for anyone. Not even you. We chose you, because you were perfect Jane. Perfect college grades. Perfect husband. Perfect health. You were destined to be one of us, and the sooner that you accept it, the sooner we can all get along. Ten Janes are supposed to be on S.J. Lane; not nine but ten. Jane, you are our ten."

"But I didn't ask to be. I never asked to be a part of your little cult or whatever it is. I never asked to be one of you!"

"No one asks, silly. They are chosen. We chose you. We took a vote."

"Why? How did you even find me?"

“We were looking for a new Jane, but technically, you found us. You inquired about my house. You were meant to be on S.J. Lane, Jane.”

“Bullshit! You gave that lady, the realtor’s card so that I would call her. You wanted her to show me that house!”

“What card?”

“You know what card I’m talking about! Your realtor’s card! Look, I just want my life back. The way that it was before buying that damn house! Before meeting all of you.”

“There’s no going back Jane. And it’s time for you to start accepting the fact that you are one of us now. You are needed. And we have plenty for you to do.” They giggled. “We will see you when you get home.”

“What don’t you get? We’re not going back to that house!”

“Oh, but you will.”

Red-Haired Jane pulled out her cell phone and turned it in my direction.

I covered my mouth as Latino Jane waved at me. She was holding a knife and standing over my parents as they slept.

“I swear, if you touch them, I will kill you!” I yelled. But she blew me a kiss.

"Oh, see, we knew that you had it in you," Blonde Jane winked. "You see, we know everything about you Jane. All of your family and your handful of friends. We know everything about your husband as well. We would hate for someone that you love to come up missing---or dead because of your disobedience. You wouldn't want that, would you?"

"They don't have anything to do with this!"

"But they have everything to do with you. We can't hurt a Jane. It's the rule. But nothing says that we can't do something not so nice to the ones that you love. Come home Jane. And no one gets hurt. Come home and join us. Come home and embrace who you are and who you were meant to be. It's all in your best interest. Jane's deserve the highest quality of life. That's what we are offering you. That's all we've been trying to give you. We'll see you at home Jane. Chao!"

Both of them wiggled their fingers and skipped out of the hotel room.

I grabbed my chest. I felt as though I was having a heart attack, but I had to find my phone. After a while, I found it on the bathroom sink, even though I knew that I hadn't left it there---along with the hotel phone and Brice's gun.

Frantically, I called my parents phone repeatedly.

Finally, on the fifth time, they answered.

"Hello?"

I exhaled and started to cry.

~***~

"Maybe the only way out, is to go through," I explained to Brice.

"They can't do this Jane! There has to be something that we can do! Someone that we can call!"

"Who? What?"

Brice shrugged his shoulders as we pulled up at home.

"Why? Why is it a must for you to become one of them? What does that even mean Jane?"

"I don't know. I don't quite understand that part either. Maybe they want something from me. I don't know what it is, but what other choice do we have? They're threatening my parents. Our families. They're messing with my job. I don't know what else to do," I moaned in defeat.

Brice was more than frustrated and I could hear it in his voice. "So, what's the plan?"

We looked around at all of the Janes standing on their front porches as though I was some kind of queen that had just arrived. As though they'd been waiting for me.

"Your guess is as good as mine."

"Let's call the police."

"That's only going to piss them off."

"Jane. We have to do something."

I opened my door. "Let's go inside."

Inside of the house, Brice inspected it from top to bottom. He rechecked the smoke detectors for microphones and he even checked a few more places just to be sure. Then he got busy with the locks that he'd bought from the hardware store. He added two new dead bolts, on both the front and the back doors, to ensure that no one uninvited could get inside. Only we had the keys to these locks for sure.

I just sat still, and quiet, until Brice came and sat beside of me.

"Everything is going to be okay. I won't let anything happen to you. I won't let them hurt you."

"They won't hurt me Brice. They can't. She said that hurting a Jane was against the rules."

"What damn rules?"

"Who knows. But that's what she said. Apparently they have a ton of rules and they vote. They vote on decisions to follow as a whole."

"Where did these people come from?"

"Here. They came from right here."

A knock startled us and we both looked at each other. Brice opened his arm and I snuggled up against his chest. I already knew that he didn't have any plans on going to the door.

But that surely hadn't stopped them from knocking. They knocked and they knocked and we just sat there and ignored them. We sat there, quietly, both in deep thought. Both clearly frustrated beyond words.

Finally, the knocking stopped, and they went away. Or at least we thought they had. But they didn't. They started to knock on the window behind us.

"Open up. It's Jane," she said.

Still yet, we didn't say a word.

~***~

"You need a paper trail. Start making reports, and then run that bitch over with your car," Charity suggested.

"They have eyes and ears in the police department. She knew that I'd called the police on her, the last time. And now that I think about it, they probably did see a body in her trunk and just overlooked it," I mumbled to Charity.

Things were slow at work. She had a few projects to finish up, but all of my clients that I'd brought to our company, had ditched me and taken their business elsewhere.

"Well, make a complaint at another police station. You just need something on paper. Something reporting harassment or something. Save anything they send you. Start recording them when they call you. And when you flip out, not only will you have reasons why, but you'll have the proof."

I was listening to her. And she was right.

"Why do you think that they want me to be a part of them so badly?"

"I don't know. Maybe they are really obsessed with being perfect, or having the perfect community. You can never be too sure of how folk's minds work. Hell, maybe they have separation anxiety. Hell, I don't know. All I know is that they are going too far."

"I know that you are tired of this and I know that you hate that you went into business with me."

"Stop it Jane. You're my friend. This is what friends are for. Now, call Brice and tell him that after work, I'm taking you to have a few drinks."

"Lord knows I need them," I laughed and I did as I was told.

The work day came to an end and Charity and I headed for an early dinner and hopefully lots of wine. I was secretly annoyed because it was so hard for me to fully let my hair down and enjoy myself the way that I wanted to. I was always checking my surroundings and always looking over my shoulder.

"Ladies, are you ready to order?"

Charity spoke.

"Sorry, but I have to take Jane's order first."

Charity and I both looked at each other.

"So, let me guess. There's a picture of my face, on a bulletin board in your breakroom too?" I asked him.

"No. But it was. A long time ago. We are required to learn the face of a new Jane. Just in case she comes in. Anything you want on the menu, you can have."

"Wait, *have*…as in, I don't have to buy it?"

"That's right."

"Even drinks?"

"As many as you won't."

"And I don't pay for anything?"

"No. It's the rule."

What the hell is up with these rules that everyone was talking about? What rules? And where in the hell are they posted?

"Can I see the rules?"

"It's in the employee handbook. Never charge a Jane. Now, what can I get for you?"

Now, by no means did I want to be "A Jane", or whatever. But for the evening and for unlimited drinks, I figured just for today, I wouldn't complain.

Over and over again, the waiter brought me drink after drink. And though he kept saying that he couldn't give them to Charity, for free, because she wasn't a Jane, I ordered drinks and food for both of us, and with no questions asked, he always brought what I asked him to.

Two hours or so later, we literally had to force ourselves to leave.

"Charity, I'm drunk."

"Me too. I'm calling a cab," she slurred. We were parked right beside each other and she wobbled to her driver's side door.

"I'm right down the street. I can make it home."

Charity didn't answer. She damn near threw herself inside of her car and started pressing buttons on her phone.

"Just get in the car with me. You can sleep it off at the house and we will come get your car in the morning."

"I'm fine. I'm calling a cab," she said as her face hit against her phone screen. Putting my stuff inside of my car,

I managed to make my way to her and pulled her to her feet.

"Come on."

Charity fussed, but finally I had her in my passenger seat and we were ready to go.

"I'm never drinking again," Charity complained.

"Me either."

I closed my eyes and opened them about five or six times. My house was literally two minutes away. I could make it. The sudden sound of thunder caused me to crank up the car in a hurry.

"Okay Charity. You ready?"

I looked over at her. She was slumped over with her head down towards her thighs. She'd passed out.

Maybe I should just call Brice to come pick us up.

Searching for my phone, I remembered that it was in the passenger seat and since I didn't see it, Charity was probably sitting on it.

Poor phone. I could only pray that it survived the pressure from Charity's cornbread fed ass.

"Alright, Jane. Come on. Just make it home."

I put the car into drive and focused.

I made it out of the parking lot and stared at the red light. It was getting darker and darker by the second and as soon as the light turned green, I pressed on the gas.

The sound of thunder bellowed, again and again, and at the sight of rain drops hitting my windshield, I started to worry.

"Please, rain. Don't pour down until I I get home."

But my prayer was too late. As soon as I'd said the words, the rain fell heavily, causing me to freak out. I could barely see where I was going. But slowly, I continued to drive. The rain didn't let up but I exhaled as I spotted a familiar house, letting me know that I was close to S.J. Lane. I inched towards the green sign, looking at it the whole time. I smiled once I read the words, and I turned my wheel.

Thump!

I slammed on the brakes.

Charity's body wobbled and I gripped the steering wheel tightly.

"What was that?"

I opened the car door. I could literally see my house, but I inched towards the front of the car.

"Please be a dog, or a cat, or something."

At the sight of a fury tail, I exhaled. But then I gasp as I saw a body; a woman's body. She still had the dog leash wrapped around her hand and both of them were lying in front of my car.

"Oh, my God! Oh, my God!"

I dropped down to my knees and started to shake her.

"Ma'am? Ma'am? Please get up. I swear, I didn't see you! You came out of nowhere! Ma'am? Can you hear me? Please say something! Can you hear me?" I shook her as I screamed. But she didn't respond. The dog wasn't moving either.

The rain started to sting my back and I started to cry.

"Please don't be dead. Please don't be dead."

Knowing that I needed to call for help, I stood up and that's when I noticed the bright car lights right behind me.

"Help!"

I heard the car door open and shut and then finally they appeared. Blonde Jane and Silent Jane.

"Hello, Jane. What happened?"

"Ugh! Not you! Anybody but you! What are you even doing here?"

"Well, we do live down this street and your car is blocking our way."

Damn. She's right.

Blonde Jane smiled and walked towards the front of my car. Silent Jane stood still.

"Jane. You hit a woman and her dog."

I started to shake my head. "She came out of nowhere. It was raining and she just came out of nowhere. Who walks a dog in the rain?"

"Maybe she was already walking it before it started to rain. Jane. I think she's dead."

I started to cry and continued to explain myself. I didn't mean to hit her. I didn't see her.

"And you have been drinking."

"What?"

"We followed you to the bar. You've been drinking."

Well of course they'd been following me. No surprise there. But she did remind me that I was full of alcohol and I shouldn't have been driving in the first place.

I looked inside of my car. Charity was still passed out.

"Driving drunk and hitting a pedestrian is serious Jane." Silent Jane finally spoke.

"I need to call my husband."

"We need to call the police."

Her words made my heart feel as though it had completely stopped beating. "I didn't mean to hit her! I swear! I didn't mean to hit her." I cried and cried and then Blonde Jane walked closer to me.

"We can help you Jane."

"What?"

"We can make this go away. Make it as though it never even happened."

The thunder sounded again, causing the rain to fall violently.

"What do you mean?"

"Join our sisterhood. Embrace being a Jane. And this goes away."

"But, but, she's dead."

"It looks that way. And unless you want to ruin your life and go to prison for driving drunk and possibly manslaughter, you need our help. You're a Jane. We can help you. We can make this go away."

I stared at her. She looked me directly in the eyes and not once did she remove the grin from her face. I knew that she was serious. I knew that she meant every word she said.

I'd always known that the Janes had some secrets, and hearing her say that she could help me get out of something like this only confirmed that my suspicions and feelings of who they were and what they could do, had been right all along.

Through the rain, I looked at both of The Janes and then back at the lady, who was still lying on the pavement, and still hadn't moved. Her dog was whimpering, but he hadn't moved from his side either.

I couldn't believe that something like this had happened! But the more and more I thought about it, I just couldn't go to jail---or prison. I wouldn't last a day.

Cars were passing by, but no one stopped.

"Time is ticking, Jane. Would you like our help? Would you like to officially join us? No wants. No worries. No problems. Just Janes."

My conscious was eating me alive. I had no idea how they would cover it up, but that wouldn't change the fact that I'd hit her and more than likely killed her.

The way that I saw it, either way my life was ruined; whether I went to jail, or if I had to become Blonde Jane's *bitch.*

"All you have to do is say yes."

Unsure of what to think or what to do, I cried harder than I ever had before. But neither of the women tried to comfort me. Both of them just stood there.

Seeing my life flash before my eyes, finally, I made a decision. I made a horrible decision.

"Do you want our help Jane?"

I took a deep breath and nodded my head.

"Yes."

"Okay. Go home Jane."

Silent Jane finally moved from where she had been standing. I watched her head to the front of my car and first she pulled the woman by her legs out of the way, and then the dog.

"Go home Jane." Blonde Jane repeated.

I continued to cry as I got into my car. Hesitantly, I turned down S.J. Lane. Charity mumbled, in her sleep as I cried my heart out.

What had I done? And why did I feel liked I'd just signed a deal with the Devil?

After minutes of figuring that I would probably die of guilt, and unsure of the hell that the Janes would more than likely put me through, I changed my mind. I'd rather see what happened as a result of my actions.

I pulled out of the driveway, and headed back towards the scene, but when I got there…they were gone.

The Janes, the woman and the dog, were gone.

~**********************~

CHAPTER SIX

"Jane, what the hell are you wearing?" Brice asked.

For three straight days, after the accident, I'd stayed in bed. Brice assumed that I was sick, but I wasn't; at least not physically. But mentally, I was going through.

I couldn't stop thinking about the accident. I saw the woman, lying lifeless, in the pouring rain, every time I closed my eyes. And of course, how could I not think about The Janes.

Surprisingly, they hadn't bothered me until the third day. Maybe they'd known that I would need time to process it all. But early that morning, while Brice was still asleep, Blonde Jane sent a text message telling me that she needed to talk to me.

Assuming that it was about the accident, and devastated that they now had something to hang over my head, I rolled out of bed and headed over to her house. She was waiting for me on her front porch. She reached me a bag full of dresses that were just my size, with matching headbands and told me that I needed to start dressing like a Jane. Though I didn't want to, I took the bag. Then she told me that I would be expected at lunch around noon.

I asked her about the accident and about the woman, but she pretended not to know what I was talking about. She looked at me with a blank stare and simply told me that everything was okay.

"Jane? Why are you dressed like them?"

I was sure that they had taken pictures or had gotten some kind of proof of the accident and of what I'd done to make sure that I played by their rules. So, at this moment, that's exactly what I was going to do.

"I'm going to lunch with the Janes," I mumbled to Brice.

"What? Really?"

"I have a plan. You got to trust me. All they've ever wanted was for me to become one of them. If I pretend to, maybe gain their trust, and who knows what I'll find out that we can use. Besides, we have time. At least until the rental is ready. By then, we need to have something," I said to him, which was partly true.

Even though they had something on me, I was sure that they'd done worse, and if I could just find out something, that would make us "even", maybe I could still have a life…without them in it.

"I don't know about this Jane. Are you sure?"

"Trust me. They won't hurt me. It's the rule. Just focus on work and I'll focus on getting our lives back on track."

I kissed him.

"Um, you do look kind of sexy, in a naughty school girl kind of way," he licked his lips.

"Oooh, then maybe I need a spanking," I forced myself to flirt back with my husband and minutes later, I forced myself to have sex with him too. I wasn't into it, at all, but he couldn't tell as I faked my way through it. My mind was on everything else, but I needed for everything between us to be okay.

After we were finished, I re-dressed, and I headed outside. All of the Janes were standing right in front of my house; waiting for me.

"You clean up so well. Ladies, Jane has finally recognized her destiny. We have a new Jane!" all of the ladies clapped.

"Okay, okay ladies, so where are we going for lunch?"

After a few more minutes of chatting, they finally decided and we all followed each other to a nearby restaurant. Apparently, one of them must have called ahead, while we were on our way, because when we got there, there was already a table waiting for us.

The waitress took our orders. I noticed that we sat far away from the other people. And I also noticed that none of the people so much as looked in our direction.

After we were settled, Blonde Jane took out a notebook. She immediately started talking.

"Let's get down to business, shall we? Jane C.?"

"We have a charity event coming. We all need to be in attendance. Donation amount, $25,000."

"Jane K.?"

"Senator Lopez got caught cheating again. Mistress handled."

"Jane M.?"

"Time to pay our husbands."

I sat in awe as Blonde Jane called on each one of them. All of them had something to say that was worse than what the Jane said before them. Finally, the last one was Silent Jane.

"Jane P.?"

"Body gone. No evidence. All is good."

Was she talking about the woman that I'd hit?

At her statement, all of the Janes looked at me.

"Jane, as you see, we have our hands in everything. We run this town…and many others. We keep order. People depend on us to keep things perfect. It's our job.

Our role. Our destiny. And in return, life for us, is good. There isn't a thing that a Jane can't have. There isn't a thing that a Jane can't do. You understand?"

I was at a loss of words. It was bigger, deeper than I thought it was. I had so many questions. I wished that I had a way to record them but I knew that reaching for my phone or my purse, at that very moment, would be too obvious.

"Your relationship with your husband is a little different than ours, so let me make this clear. He can't know anything. You don't discuss any of our business with him or he will become a liability; and I'm sure you can guess how we handle liabilities in our circle. We took a vote, he can remain your husband. Just keep him out of and away from all Jane Business. Can you do that?"

Quickly, I nodded.

"Good. Any questions?"

"Why me?"

"Why not you? As I told you, you're perfect. Just like us. Perfection is rare."

"No one is perfect."

"We are."

With all of the things that I'd just heard them say, they were far from it, but I knew that she wouldn't see things my way.

"Rules. What are the rules?"

"Oh, those are simple. Don't cross a Jane. Don't charge a Jane. Don't forget a Jane. Don't touch a Jane. Don't question a Jane. Don't kill a Jane. The end," Blonde Jane laughed.

"Plain and Simple!" All of the other Janes yelled and laughed as the drinks arrived.

"But why? Why are the Janes so important?"

"The Janes built this town. The Janes, those generations before us, saved lives, made careers, and built this city, and parts of the government on their backs and with their money. For years and years to come, for all that they've done, they could never be fully repaid. We have connections everywhere. Eyes and ears everywhere. Whoever said that the President was the most important person in America…lied. Believe me, the Janes are. And now, you are one of us."

"I---I---," I stuttered.

"You're not changing your mind on us, are you Jane? I'm sure that being a part of us is much better than going to prison. Wouldn't you agree?"

I nodded.

“But, what would I have to do?”

“One day at a time Jane. One day at a time,” Blonde Jane smiled. But I didn’t like the sound of that.

“Do you kill?” I whispered.

“If we have to,” she answered openly. And she waited for my next question.

“What is it about cherry-pie?”

She giggled. “Nothing. The Janes own a cherry orchard. So, why not make cherry pies?” All of the women nodded and from there, the conversation changed and for the rest of lunch, the Janes, chatted and everyone seemed to have a good time.

Everyone but me.

~***~

“But you love what you do,” Charity proclaimed.

I was being forced to do something that I didn’t want to do, not even a week after allowing the Janes to cover-up my accident. Blonde Jane had made it clear that having a career and being “A Jane”, was out of the question. She’d said that I always had to be available because I could never be sure when I would be needed. Whatever the hell that meant.

"I know. But no one really wants to work with me anyway and I just need a break. From everything. You can have all of my clients. Whatever paperwork I need to sign to make the business fully yours, I'll sign it."

Charity huffed. "Jane, what's really going on?"

"Nothing. I just need a change," I told her and I forced myself to hang up on her so that she wouldn't hear me get emotional.

I didn't want to be a Jane! Not the kind of Jane that they were. I just wanted to be me. I wanted my old life back. I wanted my career. I wanted to be happy. I wanted to be free.

Charity called me back, but I didn't answer.

To say that I regretted my decision to involve the Janes in my mistake, was an understatement. I was surrounded by women who murdered people, on purpose, lied for a living, cleaned up scandals and paid their husbands to stay married to them. That's not who I was. That's not who I wanted to be.

There was no way in hell that I was going to be able to do this! But I couldn't tell that to the Janes. I had to play it smart. I didn't how I was going to get out of this situation, but there had to be a way. There was always a way out.

But I couldn't help but wonder what would happen to me? If I tried to find something on the Janes, and take them down, of course my accident would come out and I would probably go down too.

"Charity called me and told me to tell you to answer the phone," Brice said walking into the living room.

"I'll call her back later."

Brice looked at me concerned.

"What's wrong Jane?"

"Nothing."

"Come on, don't lie to me. I know something has been up with you the last few days. What is it?"

I shook my head.

"Your plan isn't working out, is it? Babe, just don't worry about it. Let's just go back to the hotel. The rental should be open at the beginning of the month. I don't believe that anything bad will happen."

"Yes. It will."

"You really believe that they would hurt your parents or God forbid, try to frame you for murder or something?"

I nodded. "Yes, I do."

"Why? How can you be so sure?"

I looked at him. "Because…"

"Because what Jane?"

I opened my mouth but the sudden knock caused me to jump to my feet.

"I'll get it." I rushed to the door and opened it. There stood Red-Haired Jane. She placed one finger over her lips and then she simply turned around and walked away.

Though Brice had found the hidden microphones, obviously, somehow, they were still listening.

"What did she want?" Brice asked appearing behind me.

"Nothing, important." I mumbled.

"Oh. Okay, now let's finish our conversation. What were you going to say?" Brice asked.

Knowing that I couldn't tell him anything, I offered him something better.

"Nothing. I just need you…all of you," I said grabbing his wood. "That will make everything better," I winked naughtily at him and instantly he grinned.

And just like that, the conversation was over. At least for now anyway.

~***~

"Take a ride with me," Blonde Jane ordered.

"Where are we going?"

"To solve a problem."

I knew that I didn't have much of a choice. "Let me get my purse."

Blonde Jane waited by the door as I grabbed my things. Grabbing my phone, I remembered a conversation that I'd had with Charity, so hurriedly, I started at voice recording and placed the phone inside of my purse.

My heart was beating fast and my lips trembled as I forced myself to smile.

"Ready?"

I nodded.

Blonde Jane skipped from side to side across the street as I followed quietly behind her.

We got inside of her car and she sped down the road.

"What kind of problem are we going to solve?"

She didn't answer my question. She simply started to talk about random things. I needed her to say something that I could use.

"Do I have to do anything?"

"Jane, just relax. Everything is going to be fine."

We drove for about twenty-minutes and then we pulled up to a huge house on a lake.

"Come on," she said as she grabbed a bag from the backseat and then opened her car door.

“Oh no. Leave your purse. Wouldn’t want it to get ruined,” she said and she waited for me to place my purse in the passenger seat.

Damn it.

I followed her to the door and she simply turned the knob. I was in awe as soon as we entered the foyer. It was beautiful. Grand.

“I know. Breathtaking, isn’t it? I’ve always loved his house. Now, if only he could keep his dick in his pants.”

We entered the living room and I gasped at the woman, in a pool of blood, lying on the floor. Blonde Jane pulled gloves out of the bag that she was carrying and reached me a pair.

“Put them on and don’t take them off.”

I was frozen. It was so much blood, everywhere and I just wanted to get the hell out of there.

“What---what----what happened to her?”

“Hmm…looks like he shot her.”

“He? Who is he?”

“The Mayor.”

The Mayor?

I was sweating bullets as Blonde Jane started to move things around. I still hadn’t placed on the gloves.

"Why? Why did he kill this woman? Who is she? His mistress?"

She laughed. "No silly. This is his wife. She found out about his mistress, and was going to take everything. I guess the argument got a little heated, wouldn't you say?"

I watched her place the gun that was sitting on the edge of the table inside of a big towel, folded it and then put it in the bag.

"There we go."

She took off the dead woman's wedding ring and her earrings and placed them in the bag too.

"You see Jane, now the reporters and the media have a less important story," she said, kicking a few things off of the coffee table, and throwing a few pillows off of the couch. She stopped by the fireplace. "Yep. We should take this. Any *regular* burglar wouldn't leave this behind." She placed some piece of crystal in the bag and then she turned to smile at me. "Okay. I think that should just about do it. You ready to go?"

She laughed at my fright and walked ahead of me. I stared at the dead woman until she called my name. I rushed out of the house and hunched over outside.

Blonde Jane opened the bag in front of me, just as I started to throw up.

I couldn't begin to explain what I was thinking or feeling inside. The only thing that I was sure of was that there was no way in hell that I could do this! I couldn't be a part of something like this. I couldn't be one of them

She allowed me to finish and then she took the gloves out of my hand and dropped them along with the ones that she'd been wearing, inside of the bag. She placed the bag inside of her trunk and once we were inside of the car, she exhaled and looked at herself in the mirror. She frowned at the small spots of blood on her dress.

"Don't worry. You'll get used to it." Blonde Jane commented as she finally started to drive away.

No. I won't.

We drove in silence for a while. My thoughts and emotions were all over the place. I was scared beyond words of her…off them…of everything.

One of the three phones in Blonde Jane's cup holders started to vibrate, but she didn't answer it. Yet, it caused me to remember that my phone was still recording, hopefully, inside of my purse. Deciding that I could possibly get something, I broke my silence.

"So, what happens now? What happens with the Mayor?"

She glanced at me and beamed. “Now, he owes us one,” was all that she said, and for the rest of the ride home, she didn’t so much as bother to glance in my direction.

~***~

“I have been calling you! Why aren’t you answering any of my calls? What the hell is going on Jane? And don’t tell me that it’s nothing. I know you. Tell me!”

I’d opened the door to Charity’s screaming. Immediately, I looked past her to see if any of the Janes were looking. I stepped onto the porch, while she continued to ask questions.

“What? Why are you dressed like *them* Jane? What is it? What’s happening to you?”

I didn’t know how to answer her. I wanted to tell her that I’d hit someone. I wanted to tell her that the Janes cleaned up my mess. I wanted to tell her that I made the wrong choice. But I couldn’t. I couldn’t tell her anything.

“I’m your best friend. Talk to me.”

I exhaled. “I’m fine Charity, okay?”

Silent Jane stepped onto her porch. Instantly, my body tensed.

“I think it’s best that you don’t come around here, okay?” No. They hadn’t mentioned my friendship with Charity, yet, but I didn’t want them to. I wanted her to stay as far away from them as possible. "I'll come to visit you. Okay? Just don't come here anymore."

Charity asked what seemed like a million questions, but I didn't answer any of them and while she was still talking, I walked into my house and closed the door behind me. She banged on the door, cursing and screaming for a while and then finally, she was gone.

"Oh, God," I whined and slid down the door until I reached the floor. I put both of my hands over my mouth to silence the noise, and I cried as though I'd lost my best friend---which in a way, I felt like I just had.

I didn't want her tied up in any of my mess. It was the right thing to do. It was the best thing to do, for now.

I cried for a long while and then I turned my attention to the doorknob above my head. It was turning. Someone was twisting it back and forth. I just sat there, silently watching it, but no one ever knocked. I listened as the footsteps headed down the porch steps but I didn't get up to see who, or should I say, which, Jane it was.

I didn't care. It didn't matter.

I was stuck with them.

And it was nothing that I could do about it.

~***~

My phone vibrated continuously. It was late at night and since Brice was in bed beside of me, so I knew exactly who it was.

"Hello," I moaned.

"Hey Jane! We need you to come outside."

I rolled my eyes at the sound of Red-Haired Jane's voice.

"Why?"

She didn't answer my question. She hung up.

I laid there. I glanced at Brice who was snoring, and then I glanced at the window. Rolling out of bed, I headed towards it. Outside, the Janes were fully dressed and heading towards Blonde Jane's backyard with the candlesticks, the same way as they had once before.

I'd always wondered what they'd been doing that night, and why they'd been laughing, so I rushed to put on one of the dresses and in less than five minutes, I was out of the house and walking across the street.

My heart was racing. I had no idea what I was about to walk into, and I was scared that it was going to be some kind of bloody, gory, sacrifice or something.

But it wasn't.

To be honest, I'm not sure what to say that it was.

The candles that the Janes had been holding were placed on a table, and the Janes…well…

I looked all around me.

There was a table full of props and costumes.

Some of the Janes were wearing wigs and dressed up like several occupations; Red-Haired Jane was wearing a wig and a bloody doctor's coat. Silent Jane was dressed like a school teacher, and popping her hand with a ruler as she laughed. Latino Jane was dressed up like a cow-girl, with a noose around her neck, while another Jane pulled on the rope, tugging her in another direction. I heard one of the Janes introduce herself as "April" and there was even a Jane dressed up as a man. But that wasn't the worst of it. Several of the Janes were holding dolls. Some of them were pushing the dolls in strollers. Some of them, including Blonde Jane, were rocking the dolls back and forth, either singing a lullaby or talking to them as though the dolls were alive. And then some of them were breastfeeding the dolls---and I mean they literally, had their breast out, nipple pressed up against the doll's mouth, squeezing, as though milk was actually coming out of it.

What kind of shit is this?

I was so disturbed. I was speechless. All I could do was stand there. All I could think about was getting the hell out of there. And at that very moment, I didn't care if I had to spend the rest of my life behind bars, there was no way in hell that I was becoming A Jane.

Not now. Not ever.

~************************~

CHAPTER SEVEN

I hadn't been sleep in almost twenty-four hours. I'd been searching and looking for anything that I could find on the Janes. I'd found an address for Blonde Jane's ex-husband. I wanted to pay him a visit. I wanted to know about their divorce and I wanted to know what he knew about her and the other women.

I watched Charity call, but I didn't answer her call as Blonde Jane headed in my direction.

"Hello Jane," she smiled.

"Hello."

"I wanted to explain the other night. Often, we have a night where we can be whoever, or whatever we want to be…if we weren't a Jane."

"Why not just be them? Why not just be doctors, and mothers? Why pretend?"

"We're Janes. That's who we are. And that's who we will always be. But a girl can have an imagination, can't she?"

I didn't answer her.

"I know that this is a lot to take in. I remember how hard it was for Jane Parker. But she adjusted and in due time, so will you. You will see why things are the way that they are around here. Nights like that are needed to take off the edge; it allows us to forget our obligations, just for a while. You may not appreciate it yet, but you will."

I just stared at her.

"If I didn't think that you could handle it, I wouldn't have made you apart of this. Apart of us. We wouldn't have let you in."

"I never wanted to be in."

"But you are. You owe us your life. You owe us everything. Don't forget that."

"Believe me, I won't," I mumbled.

"Good. You called your parents this morning? Going for a visit?"

I looked at her confused. "So, you're still to our conversations?"

"We are always listening. Just until you really get the hang of how we do things. I have to make sure that we can trust you."

I was a prisoner in that house. And I just wanted out.

"I'm going to my parents for the weekend. Or is that against some kind of rule?"

"Nope. We all have parents Jane. If we need you, we know how to find you."

She wiggled her fingers and walked away.

Visiting my parents was just a cover-up for what I really planned to do. Blonde Jane's ex-husband lived in Greensboro, and because it was on the way to Charlotte, I was just using going to continue to my parents once I was done; just in case the Jane's had plans to check up on me.

Brice pulled in, just as I finished loading the car.

"I wish that you could come with me."

"Me too. But I have work to do."

I hugged his neck and then whispered in his ear. I told him what my real plans were and I told him that the Janes could still hear our conversations inside of the house, so I told him to be careful with what he said to me on the phone when he called me. Surprisingly, he didn't try to talk me out of my mission. He simply kissed me and let me go.

As I backed out of the driveway, all of the Janes were now standing on their front porch, waving at me as I drove away.

As soon as I was on the next street. I snatched off the hideous headband and threw it out of the window. I felt a sense of relief the further and further I drove away from the neighborhood and by the time that I hit the highway, all I felt was freedom.

I wished that we could just run away. But I knew that we couldn't. Not without consequences or without me losing people that we loved. Trying to find something to work in my favor was the only way. It was my only choice.

I drove in complete silence for a long time. And though I hadn't had any sleep, I was fueled with energy and hope. Hope that I would get something that could help me. Hope that Blonde Jane's ex-husband was the key.

But once I saw the signs for Greensboro, I became nervous. I didn't even know if he would talk to me and if he did, I was somewhat terrified of what he might say.

I already knew what they were capable of but what if he knew of more?

I navigated towards the address and to my surprise, I arrived at a homeless shelter. I double-checked the address and seeing that it was correct, I got out.

"Excuse me, I'm looking for Anthony?"

The older lady looked up at me. "Honey, this is a shelter. You have to have more than that."

"Anthony Jordan. He has this address listed. Maybe he works here."

"No. He's a regular here. A lot of them don't have relatives, so they list this address. I saw him outside. He has on a blue jacket."

I headed outside and found him sitting on a picnic table.

"Anthony?"

"Who are you?"

"Hi. I'm Jane."

At the mention of my name he jumped to his feet and backed away from me.

"What do you want? I haven't done anything."

"No. No. I just want to talk to you."

He looked at me confused.

"About your ex-wife. Jane."

He still seemed unsure.

"Why did you get a divorce?"

I sat on the picnic table and finally he inched towards me.

"Because…she's evil. But I'm sure that you know that already," he mumbled.

"Tell me more."

"What more is there to tell? I'd worked hard all of my life. I didn't have much family. My parents died when I was young. Left me their house and I was just working to make ends meet. And then one day, she approached me. She'd said that I was perfect, but I didn't understand what she meant. And then she offered me money. A monthly salary to be her husband. At first, I thought that she was kidding, but she wasn't. I knew that it was crazy, but I couldn't turn down that amount of money, so I agreed. Worst decision of my life."

The wind was cold and he started to sniffle.

"It wasn't long before I figured out that something was wrong with her. Even with sex. We didn't have sex until our wedding night, and I couldn't touch her…at all. She tied my hands to the top of the bed and ordered me to keep a hard-on while she basically pleased herself, by riding my *junk*. And when I tried to do it any other way, she would snap. So, I stopped asking. And I had better not try to hug her or simply touch her to show her affection. She would freak out and scrub whatever body part I touched with bleach. She was a lunatic. But other things were wrong with her. She didn't work but was always busy. She never slept. She was always awake. Always missing. I knew that something was up with her, but she barely talked to me. I was just there. She paid me to just be there. I had to pretend to go to work every day, just to get out of the house. I wasn't allowed to come home before a certain time. All of the other husbands do it too. I mean they require us to get dressed in suits and ties, for nothing. And then we just had to go away, all day, and return in the evening. At first, I thought that I could do it. The money was great but I realized that I had no quality of life. Two years had gone by and I was still in a house with a woman that I barely even knew. And to be honest, I'm pretty sure that she was some kind of psychopath or serial killer. And the rest of them too."

That comment caused my eyes to widen.

"Why do you say that?"

"I saw her one night in the kitchen. She had blood on her clothes, her hands, and her face. She was also holding a knife. It had blood all over it too. And then I saw her lick it. After that, I knew that I had to get away from her and all of her little friends. So, I told her that I wanted a divorce. She laughed, but I packed my clothes to show her that I was serious. She threatened me. Told me that if I left her that it would be the biggest mistake of my life. And well, she'd meant it."

He looked around and so did I.

"I lost everything. All at once. All of a sudden, all of the money that I'd been paid from her, that was sitting in the bank, was gone. The banks tried to tell me that they had no records of it. They acted as though I was crazy. My car was stolen and never found. My parent's house was burned to the ground. And no one would hire me. It's been years and still, no one will hire me. I have nothing. And it's all because of her."

We were both quiet for a while.

"And there's nothing. Nothing big that we can use? Against her? Nothing that you saw or can remember?"

He shook his head. "Even if you found something, the police are on her side. I guess she's cutting them a monthly check too."

After sitting for a few second longer, I stood up. I went into my purse and gave him everything that I had.

"Thank you," I said walking away.

"Ay, if I were you, I would just let it be. You don't want to end up like me," he said behind me.

"I won't," I smiled at him. "I won't."

I rushed to my car and minutes later, I was back on the highway, headed to my parent's house. I was disappointed. He hadn't said much of anything that I didn't already know. He hadn't given me anything that I could really use.

I exhaled and glanced at the car on the highway driving next to me. It had been the dog that was hanging out of the window that had caught my attention.

I looked back and forth from the dog to the road and then I sped up a little so that I could see the driver's face.

What?

She touched the dog's back and he came inside of the car and she rolled up the window. Thinking quickly, I found my phone and snapped a picture of her, and then I allowed her to pass me so that I could take a picture of her tag. Soon, her car was out of sight, but all I could do was smile.

The woman that I'd hit with my car…wasn't dead.

She was alive.

~***~

Learning that the woman was still alive, changed everything. Sure, she could testify that I'd hit her and left the scene, but that was nowhere near as bad as hitting her and killing her, while driving under the influence of alcohol.

I had no idea why she was traveling the same way that I was, but someone in Heaven must've been looking out for me.

The Janes hadn't done anything for me at all; at least not really. They'd tricked me. But yet again, they hadn't covered their tracks as well as they'd thought. And now all of the cards were in my hand and I couldn't wait to play them.

"How was your trip Jane?" Blonde Jane asked.

"It was just what I needed," I said honestly.

"Good." Blonde Jane stood there and looked at me for a while. Then, she spoke again. "Well, we have a problem to solve. And it's time for you to get our hands dirty. Let's take a ride."

"No."

She looked at me. "No?"

"No."

I could see that the wheels in her head were starting to turn. Maybe I should keep what I knew to myself for a while and stay onboard.

"I'm just so tired Jane. I just want to relax for a little while."

She stared at me and then she shrugged. "Okay." And with that she skipped next door to Silent Jane's house.

Brice greeted me at the door.

He hugged and kissed me but we both knew that they were listening so we didn't say much aloud. I found a piece of paper and a pen. I wrote something on it and Brice read it. I finally told him that I'd hit a woman with my car.

"What!"

I placed my finger over my lips and then I wrote a few more sentences, telling him that the woman that I hit was still alive and that the Janes had been using my guilt to make me one of them.

Brice wrote that enough was enough and told me that it was time to get the police involved.

Speaking of the Police.

I watched them walk towards our porch and up our steps. A few seconds later, they knocked.

Brice answered the door and I stood behind him.

"How can I help you?"

"Are you Jane? Jane Adams?"

I nodded.

"We need you to come down to the station."

"Why?"

"We need to ask you a few questions about Anthony Jordan."

Brice looked at me.

"What about him?"

"Did you see him recently?"

"Yes. At the shelter. We had a talk. Why? What's wrong?"

The officer looked at me.

"He's dead."

~***************************~

CHAPTER EIGHT

"So, he was alive when you spoke to him?"

"Yes. He was alive. I wouldn't have been able to speak to him if he was dead. Duh."

"Hey, I suggest you lose the attitude. You are in no position to come off like a smart ass."

"I'm innocent."

"If you're so innocent, explain your prints on the murder weapon."

"It was planted there."

"By who?"

"We both already know the answer to that."

"By who?"

"By the Janes. Who knows which one. Do you know which one?"

The Janes must've followed me to the shelter after all because Blonde Jane's ex-husband Anthony was dead, and the knife that he'd been stabbed with, was the one that had my fingerprints all over it.

"Mrs. Adams, why did you go visit the deceased?"

"I've answered this already." I'd been at the police station for 16 hours, and I'd been questioned over and over again. Our lawyer had been out of town when he got the call so we were waiting on him to show up.

"Answer it again."

"I went to see what I could find out."

"About who?"

"Blonde Jane. I mean, Jane Peterson. His ex-wife."

"Why?"

"Because talking to someone isn't a crime. Look, as I said, I didn't do anything. And I most definitely didn't kill him."

"We have a murder weapon."

"I didn't murder anyone."

"Confess and make this easy on yourself."

"We both know that The Janes did this."

"You're a Jane."

"But I'm nothing like the rest of them. But you know that already," I growled and just as I finished my sentence, our lawyer, Randy, walked it.

He told me that it was time to go.

"You know, the shelter stated that they weren't "recording" at the time of the murder. But I made a call, to a family friend, who just happens to own a business on the same street. And what do you see?"

Randy played a video on his phone. Sure enough, Blonde Jane's car pulled into the shelter's parking lot.

"What are you showing me?"

"That's Blonde Jane's…Jane Peterson's car," I blurted at him.

"That could be anyone's car," the officer said.

Randy chuckled. "Wait for it." The video played a while longer and Blonde Jane rode around to the back of the shelter, giving a different angle of her car, which it showed her license plate. Randy then showed the officer a picture with the tag blown up and then he flipped to the next photo to where it showed that the tag was registered to Jane Peterson.

"Now, why on earth would Jane Peterson be at the crime scene? The same day of the crime? At the same time that my client was there?"

"Because she set me up."

"My thoughts exactly. And if you want to make this case bigger than what it needs to be and drag this police department down with it, I suggest you pursue other suspects."

At that comment, I stood up.

"We still have a murder weapon."

"With no witnesses. And a woman on the scene who has been in my clients house, several times, where she could have easily taken a knife from her kitchen with her prints on it. And from what I hear, there has been a few favors done around here and my client caught a conversation on her cell phone, if I'm not mistaken," Randy said. I nodded. Although it was nothing that could really help us, the police officer didn't need to know that.

"That's all for now Mrs. Adams. But stay around."

I rolled my eyes and Randy led me into the hallway. Brice was waiting for me.

"Are you okay?"

"Yes."

The three of us rushed outside, and what do you know…Blonde Jane was headed inside. She looked at me confused.

"You have to try better than that," I commented to her.

"That was just a little taste of what's to come. Did you not think that we would find out that you were snooping and going to talk to my ex-husband? I should've known that we wouldn't be able to trust you."

"Whatever Jane. Better luck next time."

"Oh, don't worry. I don't need luck when the law is on my side. I'm sure that they would love to hear about your little hit and run incident. Either way, you're going down for murder."

I reached for my purse from and found my phone.

"Oh, really? The funny thing is, she isn't dead," I said to her showing her the picture of the woman and her dog. And with that, we left her standing there with a smug look on her face.

Immediately, I called my parents and told them to get out of the house and head to my brother's house, while Randy put a call into Charlotte's police department for a patrol favor.

"Okay. They're going to patrol your brother's house for a few days until we figure out if any other actions need to be taken. We just witnessed what we are dealing with here. Had that video not surfaced, things could have gone a lot different. My advice, get out of that house and away from those women" Randy said goodbye and headed to his car.

"They played the only card that they had, the knife with your hand prints on it. That's over. So, now we are leaving---"

The sudden boom caused use to jump and all of the officers that were outside, ran towards our lawyer's car, which was now up in flames.

We could hear his agonizing screams and I covered my mouth as they tried to get to him but they couldn't. Brice grabbed me and pushed my face into his chest as I started to wail.

"Brice do something!"

"I can't Jane! I can't!

Soon, Randy's screams stopped and the chatter and panic all around us was all that was left. I remained in Brice's arms as I looked back at the fire. Randy was dead. Through my tears, I glanced towards the doors of the police station. Blonde Jane just stood there. She smirked and then she placed on a pair of sunglasses, all though it was cold, and she walked away.

And just like that, the Janes strike again.

And no one was going to do a thing about it.

~***~

"Is that all of the boxes?"

"Yep."

I exhaled with relief. The rental house had finally come open and Brice and I were all moved in. It had been two weeks since Randy had been killed and since we'd been away from S.J. Lane. And we were never going back. We were back in Raleigh, and so far, so good.

We hadn't seen or heard from the Janes. We hadn't even gone to the house to move our own things. We'd paid someone to do it. And then we'd had them to drop off everything to a storage unit; we didn't want to give them our address, just in case one of them had made a deal with a Jane. And then Brice and all of his friends moved our things from the storage unit themselves.

My parents were still safe at my brother's house and were even considering staying with long term to help him and his wife with their kids. The Janes hadn't called my phone or anything and though I doubted that they'd just forgotten about me, they had nothing on me, so hopefully they'd just let me go.

Brice said goodbye to all of his buddies and once I heard him close the door, I came down the stairs.

"I really like this house."

"Good. Hopefully we can stay here for a while," Brice embraced me and I kissed his lips.

"Brice."

He looked back at me.

"Did you leave the back door open?"

He turned to look at it and then headed towards it.

But…

The sound caused me to scream as Brice hit the ground. I wanted to run towards him but I couldn't. My feet wouldn't move. For a second too long I was stuck. Finally, I screamed for him and just as I started to run in his direction, something hit me in the back of my head, hard, and in slow motion, I fell to the ground.

And instantly…everything was dark. Everything was quiet.

~***~

I opened my eyes.

Two Janes were holding me up on each side. Immediately, I started to struggle, but they wouldn't let me go.

"Brice! Where is my husband?"

"He's dead," I heard her voice from behind me.

Seconds later, Blonde Jane appeared in front of me. All of the other Janes were sitting in her back yard, looking on.

"I hate that we couldn't be friends, Jane. I tried. We all tried. I guess, some people just don't know a good thing when they see it. Some people are just so ungrateful! I mean, really. Did you think that we were just going to let you go? Did you think that betraying your "sisters" wouldn't come with consequences?"

"You…are not…my sister! Let me go!"

"Nope. You see, at first, it was all in good fun, but I saw potential in you. I checked you out. I thought you would make the perfect Jane. But I was wrong."

"Good fun? What are you talking about?"

"Where is this recording? The one that you told the police that you have? What's on it? Who has it? And who has seen it?"

"Wouldn't you like to know?"

"Tell me what's on it. Where is it?"

"We checked your phone, it wasn't there. So, where is it? Did you send it to someone? Who? What's on this so-called recording?"

"I'm not telling you shit!"

She raised her hand as though she wanted to slap me, but she didn't.

"Fine. Don't tell me. It's not like you'll ever get to use it," she said and I watched Latino Jane hold out her hand, and Blonde Jane placed a gun inside of it.

I started to panic and tried to break free, but I couldn't. Blonde Jane walked towards me. I huffed and tried to catch my breath.

"You were just too nosey for your own good. You're a stubborn little thing too. And you ask a lot of questions.

You don't know how to just go with the flow Jane. You would've never fit in anyway."

Latino Jane eyed the gun and then she looked at me.

"I thought killing a Jane was against the rules," I growled in an attempt to change her mind.

"It is. I'm not going to kill you Jane. She is."

I hadn't noticed Charity sitting in the very back of the crowd until she stood up.

What?

She walked towards me and Latino Jane handed her the gun.

"Charity, help me!"

I screamed at her but, she didn't say anything.

"Charity? What are you doing?"

"You know, you've always been perfect Jane. Even in college. You had the perfect grades. The perfect hair. The perfect guy," Charity mumbled.

My heart filled up with anger as Charity continued to speak. "But we were friends. You were my best friend. Hell, you were my only friend. I was always trying to be like you, but most of the time you were too busy basking in your own glory, to see that I admired you. But I did. I looked up to you. And then, you just, got too busy for me.

You stopped taking my calls. You changed your number and moved. You were just gone."

"Charity, it wasn't like that and you know it," I forced myself to try to speak to her calmly. "We got busy. We all got busy; including you! I was busy running my own company! You of all, people know how that is!"

"Yes. I do. But I needed you Jane. When I married a man, who beat me just because it was cold outside, I needed you. Every time I covered up a black-eye, I needed you. When I had my first and my second miscarriage, from being thrown to the ground and stomped, I needed you. I needed my best friend, my only friend, during my divorce and during the birth of my child, but you weren't there. You were never there. And then I saw you. At the convention, looking better than ever. You were glowing. You looked so happy. You looked perfect. And though I was hoping that it was all just for show, it wasn't. You'd just married the man of your dreams. Your business was doing great. You were still as perfect as you'd always been. And I hated it. I hated you."

She pointed the gun at me.

"Charity. Put the gun down. It's me. Jane. Your friend."

"Just being in your presence made my skin crawl. Every time Brice called you or when you smiled at one of his text messages, I was overtaken by envy. You had the perfect life. And what did I have? Other than scars, a career that I'd only gotten into because of you, and a child that reminded me so much of his father that I could hardly look at him. What else did I have?"

"You have me Charity. We're best friends."

She didn't comment to what I'd said. She just continued to ramble. "I remembered when my ex-husband would get drunk. He was one of those men who had everything in the world, but it still wasn't enough. He would get drunk, and complain. He would complain about his life and lack of love and support from his family. He would complain about Jane."

She nodded in Blonde Jane's direction.

Wait. What?

"My ex-husband is her brother."

What the hell?

"He would be so drunk that he would talk about the Janes and what they did. He would tell family secrets and he would complain that his family, his parents, always loved her more. Always treated her like she was special and like he was an accident. He talked about all of their dirty laundry. He called the Janes evil and bullies and said that they thought that they were perfect, but in reality, they were nothing. And then he would beat me, and then sober up and forget everything that he'd said. But I never forgot. Though my ex-husband had never introduced me to his family, because he hated them, I went on a search for this sister of his that he despised so much, and it led me to S.J. Lane. One day, I drove by. No one was out, but I did see that there was a house open on that street. And then I had an idea. If these "Janes" were as awful as my ex-husband said that they were, then it was only necessary to send you into the lion's den? Your fairytale of a life didn't deserve the perfect ending. It was time for someone else to have it for a change. Of course, I knew that you were looking for a house, and just from viewing the pictures online, I knew that you would love it. I called the realtor on the sign and she immediately told me that my name had to be Jane in order for her to even show the house to me. I told her that I had a sister, named Jane, that was interested, and I went to pick up one of her cards direction. I told her that I would be sending you in her direction and I even sweetened the deal by telling her that if she got you to buy the house that, not only would she get her commission, but I would give her a handsome sum out of my divorce slash hush money settlement, to last her for a very long time. And then, I found the young woman, outside of the coffee shop, and paid her to give the realtor's card."

My mouth opened wide. I couldn't believe what I was hearing. I couldn't believe that Charity had been a part of some of this from the very beginning.

"I didn't kill her though. I didn't even know that she was missing until you said something about it. So, that wasn't me. I just needed to get you on that lane. I even had a hand in the break-ins near your condos. Anything to push you towards moving. And it worked. And then the realtor did her part with getting you to buy the house."

Blonde Jane seemed to be enjoying the show. She was enjoying the fact that I was in shock and that I'd been deceived.

"Once you got the house, I drove by one day before you moved in. Of course, Blonde Jane came outside to inquire about my visit. I introduced myself to her for the first time. She asked about her brother whom she hadn't seen in years, after getting him the top seat at a multi-million-dollar company. At the time, I didn't want to tell her how much he hated her guts, so I didn't. I told her what she wanted to know and then I asked her for a favor. I told her that her brother had slightly mentioned some of their "practices" and I asked her to make your life a living hell, just for a little while. Just for fun. Of course, she hadn't revealed any of her real motives to me, she simply told me that she would see what she could do. I'd known from her brother that they could be real bitches and even a little crazy, but I didn't know how true all of it was until you started to tell me what they were doing to you. I was delighted inside. Finally, your life wasn't so perfect anymore. Finally, you didn't have it all together. Finally, you weren't better than me."

I guess it's true when they say that sometimes your biggest enemies, are those that are closest and dearest to you. And usually by the time that you notice, it's always too late.

At this point, I'd been swallowed by rage and if I could just break free and get ahold of Charity, I would have choked the shit out of her!

"You encouraged me. You encouraged me to leave so many times!"

"I had to play a role. But you're stubborn. I knew that you wouldn't listen. I also made sure that your condo sold so that you wouldn't change your mind and go back there."

My feelings were crushed. It just goes to show that you never truly know someone and you would be surprised at what people really feel about you.

"The young woman was the girl in your trunk, wasn't she?" I asked Blonde Jane. But she shook her head no.

"I didn't know anything about this. That was "garbage control" for the Lieutenant at the police station. His drug addict daughter was the girl in my trunk that day. Whoever this woman is, we didn't have anything to do with that." Blonde Jane admitted. I knew that I'd seen an arm in her trunk! I knew it! I assumed that the police had been ordered to overlook the body.

"And as I said, I didn't do anything to her either. So, maybe something else happened to her." Charity walked closer to me with the gun still in her hand. "I never planned to kill you. I just wanted you to suffer. I just wanted them to make your life a living hell. But, now, I don't have a choice. I have to think about the safety of my son."

"That's what you get for making a deal with the Devil! Seriously, Charity, do you think that they are just going to let you walk out of here after you shoot me?"

Charity looked as though she was thinking about my statement.

"Think about it. You'll know too much about them. Do you think that they aren't going to take care of you too?"

Charity looked at Blonde Jane who was simply smiling at her. I could tell that Charity was unsure of what her smile meant.

"Shut up Jane! You're just trying to confuse me."

"And your son? She wouldn't hurt your son. That's her nephew."

"Are you sure about that Jane?" Blonde Jane asked me. "Our views on family are slightly different. The Janes are my family---first. Everything and everyone else comes after. But my decisions will always benefit us; even if they are some hard decisions to make. Even if they include family," she said.

"You're just evil!" I screamed at her.

"Thank you. Thank you very much. Now, Charity, Shoot her."

"No Charity. Make her shoot me herself."

"Oh, believe me, if I could. I would. But you know the rules. And we pride ourselves on following the rules around here Jane. But of course, you wouldn't know anything about that."

"Who cares about your stupid rules? Charity even if they let you go, they will own you. They will always have this hanging over your head and you will always belong to them. Think about it. If they'll try to do it to me, surely, they'll do it to you. She could've handled this herself, yet she called you to do it. It's about power. And control. They crave it. They think that they deserve it. They just want to have something to hold against you."

"Shoot her," Blonde Jane repeated bluntly. All of the other Janes looked on quietly, but attentively. None of them said a word. Charity's hands began to shake.

She looked at me. I could tell from the look on her face that she was changing her mind. I could tell that she truly hadn't meant for things to go this far. I could tell that she was sorry. And I could also tell that she knew that if she didn't shoot me, that she would have to deal with the consequences.

"Shoot her!" Blonde Jane yelled again. But Charity still didn't pull the trigger. Instead, she lowered the gun.

"No."

"No?" Blonde Jane repeated.

"No."

Charity dropped the gun and as soon as it hit the ground, she was shot down.

"No!" I screamed as I looked in the direction of Red-Haired Jane who was still holding the smoking gun. She walked over to Charity and kicked her, but Charity didn't move.

"See Jane, now that was your fault! You couldn't just shut up and take the bullet. You talk too much," Blonde Jane said. I didn't respond. Instead, I stared at Charity.

"Well, I guess, rules are made to be broken," Blonde Jane spoke to Red-Haired Jane who turned the gun on me. But just as she pointed it, another shot ranged through the air and she clutched her shoulder.

"Drop your weapon!"

To my surprise, Mr. Peterson, Blonde Jane's husband, came from out of the house and inched towards us.

"What are you doing? Why are you even here?" Blonde Jane scowled her husband. But he didn't answer her. All of the Janes stood up and Latino Jane rushed towards Charity, picked up the gun, and immediately, he turned his gun on her.

"Drop it!" He screamed at her.

I watched Blonde Jane inch closer and closer to the shovel that was lying up against the house, as Mr. Peterson focused on Latino Jane.

"What are you doing stupid? Put the gun down and go back into the house! You're starting to piss me off! I don't pay you to be a hero. I pay you to listen!" Blonde Jane screamed at him, but still he ignored her.

"I'm warning you. Drop your weapon!" He continued to scream at the Latino Jane who wasn't the least bit frightened or bothered by his threats. She was actually smiling at him.

I continued to watch Blonde Jane. Keeping her eyes on her husband the whole time, she finally made it to the shovel and just as her finger tips touched the shovel's handle, I screamed.

"Watch out!" But another gunshot caused Blonde Jane to freeze.

"I wouldn't do that if were you," Silent Jane was the one holding the gun this time. Everybody looked around confused and then seconds later the S.W.A.T. team came running from every direction.

What just happened?

The Janes loosened their grip on me and I pulled away from them as the men with guns surrounded them. Blonde Jane was staring at Silent Jane as she walked closer to us.

"What is your problem?" Blonde Jane asked her.

"You. My problem has always been you and this entire organization, if that's what you want to call it. I'm F.B.I. Agent Stephanie Mills. I've been an undercover Jane for five years. And this is Jimmy Ricardo, from Internal Affairs. Who has also been undercover with me every step of the way," she nodded at Mr. Peterson.

"You were a cop?" Blonde Jane asked both of them at the same time. Well, I'll be damned! I was speechless.

"We've known about your practices for years. "The Janes". We'd heard so many stories, but taking it all down was a change. And your police department is corrupted, so we couldn't lean on them for help. So, we had to work harder and smarter. For five long years, we've built a case on you---on all of you. Dating back at least twenty years and three generations of Janes. And every police officer, judge, mayor, doctor, politician, pastor, everyone that you have ever done a "job" for, everyone that The Janes have ever solved a problem for, are all going down. We wanted to catch everyone involved, that's why we took our time. And finally, we had enough. Finally, we could make our move."

Blonde Jane was still in disbelief. "This is impossible! We checked you out. We searched your background and read all of your files. You were perfect."

"I was, wasn't I? Thank you. I wrote it all myself. But it was all fake. Every last word of it, was a lie."

"Have you forgotten? You've done things too. And you know that I know about the things that you've done," Blonde Jane smirked at her.

"Or at least the things that you thought I done. All of my "duties" over the years were never actually taken care of, at least not to your standards. I always found a way around them. The ones that I was ordered to kill, I put them in protective services for the time being. And anytime that I was supposed to get rid of a body for you, it went straight to evidence. Sorry, but my hands are still clean. I was always doing my job. The right way. Not the Janes way. You were just too busy to pay attention. Remember that husband of mine that died months after I moved in? That was Special Agent Fargo. He never died. We staged the whole thing so that I could earn your sympathy; what little you had to give. But it forced you to lay off of me in the beginning, making it easier for me to "become a part" of the group, without you constantly watching me."

I never would've guessed that Silent Jane was F.B.I. Never in a million years.

"Even the Jane that "died" from cancer, you know, the one who lived in this house before you moved here…she's still alive. She helped us tremendously with our case. She hated how you treated her and sold you and plenty of people out a long time ago. Though she was born and raised "A Jane", from the moment I saw her, I knew that she was the one that I would be able to get to turn on the group. So, we faked her diagnosis, and her death. She's safe. She's free. While the rest of you, will spend the rest of your lives in prison. Nice chatting with you. Now, get them the hell out of here," Silent Jane commanded and wiggled her fingers.

Blonde Jane yelled and made threats but they led her and all of the other Janes out of the backyard in handcuffs.

I touched Charity. She wasn't moving and despite what she'd done to me, my heart broke knowing that she was dead.

"I always knew that you wouldn't become one of them. I was rooting for you from the very beginning."

I looked at Silent Jane---well Stephanie.

"For a second, I thought that I wouldn't have a choice; especially after the hit and run."

"Jane Peterson, or the Blonde Jane as you call her, staged that. We'd followed you to the bar. We knew that you'd been drinking. She made a call as soon as you pulled out of the parking lot. She'd had her standing in the rain, waiting on you to try to turn and then she was to throw herself in front of your car, with the dog on the right side to lessen the impact. She never died. She's alive. Her dog is too."

I knew that already. I just couldn't believe how far Blonde Jane had gone to try to turn me into one of them. And it almost worked.

"She was paid handsomely and told to disappear. Blonde Jane only wanted you to think that you'd killed her. She knew that the Janes "saving you" would be the only way to get you to become a part of the team. Since nothing else had worked of course."

"So, all of this was…"

"You were simply the wrong Jane, on the wrong lane," she said. "Granted your friend sent you in this direction, any Jane, that got in that house, they would've done the same thing. They would've tried to convert them too. Considering that they screened backgrounds, if she was up to their standards, they would have seen it as destiny for her to be one of them. Don't take this the wrong way, there was nothing special about you---except that all of your life you'd managed to do things right. And that was a plus for them. They really believed that they were "chosen" and that they were better. It's all that they knew. It's what they'd been taught from their mothers, and their grandmothers, who had all been taught the same exact thing. That's *why* you. You often asked that question but there was no special answer."

The man that was called Mr. Peterson appeared with the EMT and the rushed towards Charity.

"I couldn't stop them from shooting her. I had to wait on the team to get here. Had I blown my cover too soon, things could have turned out pretty bad," she said and I wept as they covered Charity's face with a sheet.

"You put up one hell of a fight. I was protecting you, even when you didn't know it." She helped me up and she told one of the workers to look at my head. She waited for me and once they were done, she walked with me out of the backyard. The entire lane was filled with police cars, and there were so many people going in and out of all of the Jane's houses.

"Someone is waiting for you. He refused to go to the hospital without you," she pointed at the ambulance. I could see Brice lying inside.

"Goodbye Jane. Take care," she yelled after me as I ran to him. The worker closed the door to the ambulance behind me and I exhaled and cried at the sight of Brice's chest.

~***~

Six Months Later…

“Brice, catch him,” I said as Roman, Charity’s son, ran around the car. She’d named me beneficiary on all of her things and since she was her son’s custodial parent, in the eyes of the court, she’d designated me to take care of him if something ever happened to her. With no fight from her ex-husband who didn’t even want him, we took Charity’s son Roman home…as our son.

“I gotcha’!” Brice yelled as he tickled him.

I smiled at them. “Come on. She’s waiting for us.”

We walked towards the realtor who was waiting for us on the front steps. Our house on S.J. Lane had been sold, along with all of the rest, to a company that was building a new shopping center in that area.

Finally, we were looking to buy a new house, in Raleigh; and the only problem was that we couldn’t go further away from Smithfield. We’d just found out that we were three months pregnant and we needed to get settled…soon.

But this time, my approach was different. I’d researched the house, the neighborhood, the owners, and even the realtor that was showing the house to us. I learned the hard way that u just could never be too sure. But all was well, and we were hoping that this house was a winner.

“Hello, you must be Brice,” she said and shook his hand. And then she turned and looked at me. “And you must be Mary Jane? Or just Jane?”

I shook my head. “No. It’s just Mary. Please just call me Mary,” I replied, cringing at the sound of that name.

~*********************************~

THE END

THANKS FOR READING! CHECK OUT MORE OF MY BOOKS AND JOIN MY FACEBOOK GROUP AT:

https://www.facebook.com/groups/authorbmhardin/

LIST OF BOOKS:

THE HIDDEN WIFE

THE WRONG HUSBAND

YOUR PASTOR, MY HUSBAND

DESPERATE

AND MANY MORE!